Black Towers to Danger

3·23-14

SELECTED FICTION WORKS BY
L. RON HUBBARD

FANTASY
The Case of the Friendly Corpse
Death's Deputy
Fear
The Ghoul
The Indigestible Triton
Slaves of Sleep & The Masters of Sleep
Typewriter in the Sky
The Ultimate Adventure

SCIENCE FICTION
Battlefield Earth
The Conquest of Space
The End Is Not Yet
Final Blackout
The Kilkenny Cats
The Kingslayer
The Mission Earth Dekalogy*
Ole Doc Methuselah
To the Stars

ADVENTURE
The Hell Job series

WESTERN
Buckskin Brigades
Empty Saddles
Guns of Mark Jardine
Hot Lead Payoff

A full list of L. Ron Hubbard's
novellas and short stories is provided at the back.

*Dekalogy—a group of ten volumes

L. RON HUBBARD

Black Towers to Danger

GALAXY
PRESS

Published by
Galaxy Press, LLC
7051 Hollywood Boulevard, Suite 200
Hollywood, CA 90028

Printed in the United States of America.

ISBN-10 1-59212-257-4
ISBN-13 978-1-59212-257-8

Library of Congress Control Number: 2007903614

Contents

Stories from Pulp Fiction's Golden Age

A ND it *was* a golden age.
The 1930s and 1940s were a vibrant, seminal time for a gigantic audience of eager readers, probably the largest per capita audience of readers in American history. The magazine racks were chock-full of publications with ragged trims, garish cover art, cheap brown pulp paper, low cover prices—and the most excitement you could hold in your hands.

"Pulp" magazines, named for their rough-cut, pulpwood paper, were a vehicle for more amazing tales than Scheherazade could have told in a million and one nights. Set apart from higher-class "slick" magazines, printed on fancy glossy paper with quality artwork and superior production values, the pulps were for the "rest of us," adventure story after adventure story for people who liked to *read*. Pulp fiction authors were no-holds-barred entertainers—real storytellers. They were more interested in a thrilling plot twist, a horrific villain or a white-knuckle adventure than they were in lavish prose or convoluted metaphors.

The sheer volume of tales released during this wondrous golden age remains unmatched in any other period of literary history—hundreds of thousands of published stories in over nine hundred different magazines. Some titles lasted only an issue or two; many magazines succumbed to paper shortages during World War II, while others endured for decades yet. Pulp fiction remains as a treasure trove of stories you can read, stories you can love, stories you can remember. The stories were driven by plot and character, with grand heroes, terrible villains, beautiful damsels (often in distress), diabolical plots, amazing places, breathless romances. The readers wanted to be taken beyond the mundane, to live adventures far removed from their ordinary lives—and the pulps rarely failed to deliver.

In that regard, pulp fiction stands in the tradition of all memorable literature. For as history has shown, good stories are much more than fancy prose. William Shakespeare, Charles Dickens, Jules Verne, Alexandre Dumas—many of the greatest literary figures wrote their fiction for the readers, not simply literary colleagues and academic admirers. And writers for pulp magazines were no exception. These publications reached an audience that dwarfed the circulations of today's short story magazines. Issues of the pulps were scooped up and read by over thirty million avid readers each month.

Because pulp fiction writers were often paid no more than a cent a word, they had to become prolific or starve. They also had to write aggressively. As Richard Kyle, publisher and editor of *Argosy*, the first and most long-lived of the pulps, so pointedly explained: "The pulp magazine writers, the best of them, worked for markets that did not write for critics or attempt to satisfy timid advertisers. Not having to answer to anyone other than their readers, they wrote about human beings on the edges of the unknown, in those new lands the future would explore. They wrote for what we would become, not for what we had already been."

Some of the more lasting names that graced the pulps include H. P. Lovecraft, Edgar Rice Burroughs, Robert E. Howard, Max Brand, Louis L'Amour, Elmore Leonard, Dashiell Hammett, Raymond Chandler, Erle Stanley Gardner, John D. MacDonald, Ray Bradbury, Isaac Asimov, Robert Heinlein—and, of course, L. Ron Hubbard.

In a word, he was among the most prolific and popular writers of the era. He was also the most enduring—hence this series—and certainly among the most legendary. It all began only months after he first tried his hand at fiction, with L. Ron Hubbard tales appearing in *Thrilling Adventures, Argosy, Five-Novels Monthly, Detective Fiction Weekly, Top-Notch, Texas Ranger, War Birds, Western Stories,* even *Romantic Range.* He could write on any subject, in any genre, from jungle explorers to deep-sea divers, from G-men and gangsters, cowboys and flying aces to mountain climbers, hard-boiled detectives and spies. But he really began to shine when he turned his talent to science fiction and fantasy of which he authored nearly fifty novels or novelettes to forever change the shape of those genres.

Following in the tradition of such famed authors as Herman Melville, Mark Twain, Jack London and Ernest Hemingway, Ron Hubbard actually lived adventures that his own characters would have admired—as an ethnologist among primitive tribes, as prospector and engineer in hostile climes, as a captain of vessels on four oceans. He even wrote a series of articles for *Argosy,* called "Hell Job," in which he lived and told of the most dangerous professions a man could put his hand to.

Finally, and just for good measure, he was also an accomplished photographer, artist, filmmaker, musician and educator. But he was first and foremost a *writer,* and that's the L. Ron Hubbard we come to know through the pages of this volume.

This library of Stories from the Golden Age presents the best of L. Ron Hubbard's fiction from the heyday of storytelling, the Golden Age of the pulp magazines. In these eighty volumes, readers are treated to a full banquet of 153 stories, a kaleidoscope of tales representing every imaginable genre: science fiction, fantasy, western, mystery, thriller, horror, even romance—action of all kinds and in all places.

Because the pulps themselves were printed on such inexpensive paper with high acid content, issues were not meant to endure. As the years go by, the original issues of every pulp from *Argosy* through *Zeppelin Stories* continue crumbling into brittle, brown dust. This library preserves the L. Ron Hubbard tales from that era, presented with a distinctive look that brings back the nostalgic flavor of those times.

L. Ron Hubbard's Stories from the Golden Age has something for every taste, every reader. These tales will return you to a time when fiction was good clean entertainment and the most fun a kid could have on a rainy afternoon or the best thing an adult could enjoy after a long day at work.

Pick up a volume, and remember what reading is supposed to be all about. Remember curling up with a *great story.*

—Kevin J. Anderson

KEVIN J. ANDERSON *is the author of more than ninety critically acclaimed works of speculative fiction, including The Saga of Seven Suns, the continuation of the Dune Chronicles with Brian Herbert, and his* New York Times *bestselling novelization of L. Ron Hubbard's* Ai! Pedrito!

Black Towers to Danger

CHAPTER ONE

Hostility from Camp Jaguar

BILL MURPHY had no premonition of danger when he turned down the slimy trail which wandered through the engulfing jungle above Lake Maracaibo.

He pulled up on his small horse, hooked the reins around the horn and wiped the sweat from his hands. Casually he began to build a cigarette.

He was not hurried about it. He had lots of time and he liked the flavor of his mission.

For two days Marcia Stewart had been at Camp Jaguar getting her late father's affairs in good order. It was time Bill Murphy made his call. He wondered if Marcia still thought that way about him. He hoped her dad wouldn't leave his ghost on the premises. Old man Stewart had been an oilman of the old hard school, a fighter to the last ditch. Now that he was gone, things ought to be fairly calm in Venezuela.

Unable to light a match, Bill removed his sunhat and ran the match through his hair to dry it. That done, he applied the flame to the cigarette.

The white helmet flew high and to the right.

The explosion came an instant later.

Bill Murphy had heard the shrill whine of the bullet.

Hastily he swung his mount into the shelter of a bush,

stepped off and hauled a Springfield from its boot. He went down into the muck on his hands and knees and crawled out for a better view.

A slug kicked splattering mud into his face.

"Damn," said Bill, unemotionally. He looked at his ruined white shirt and said "Damn," again.

He went around the other side of the bush, found himself still in shelter, crawled another ten feet and got a clear view of the enemy.

"Injun," said Bill.

He threw off the safety catch, sighted down the barrel through the number ten peep.

The Indian's black hair was glistening in a stray beam of sunlight. The cruel profile was set in a waiting expression.

Bill squeezed the trigger.

The Indian flipped backwards, his gun went up into the air and lit across his body.

Bill Murphy walked over to the clearing, leading his horse. He turned the body over with his foot.

"Camp Jaguar man," said Bill, in a disinterested fashion.

He sighed again and looked at his own muddy shirt which had so lately been stiff with starch for Marcia's benefit. Well, Marcia wouldn't love him the less for a dirty shirt if she loved him at all.

Bill swabbed the sweat from his forehead, inspected the hole in the sun helmet, replaced it. He mounted and headed down the twilight trail again with the flies buzzing around his head in pursuit formation.

4

"Dum de da de da," said Bill, thinking about Marcia again.

"Have to do something about these yellow devils," said Bill to his horse.

"Gettin' so it ain't safe to ride five miles from camp without having to waste ammunition on them. . . . Wonder if Marcia looks different."

He was drowsy with the heat and his great shoulders drooped forward a little. He was riding like a sack of meal when he came in sight of the oil derricks of Camp Jaguar.

The place hadn't changed much in the last two months. Old man Stewart was dead but the wells were still going down.

"Hello, Romano," said Bill. "Where's Marcia?"

Romano had been sitting on a rock with a rifle across his knees. He glanced angrily up at the machine-gun tower and saw that the guard was asleep.

Romano turned deliberately around. He hefted his rifle. His face was as thin as a dagger blade and his hair was very black. His skin had a yellow cast to it like an Indian's, but Romano claimed to be pure Castilian.

His eyes were squinted up.

"You better get the hell out of here, *amigo,*" said Romano.

"What's the matter?" said Bill, rolling another cigarette and cocking a heel over the saddle.

"You know what's the matter," said Romano.

"Where's Marcia?"

Bill pulled a match from his sweat-stained pocket, rubbed it through his hair and lighted his smoke. He peered through the smoke haze at Romano.

5

"She don't want to see anything of you," said Romano, definitely.

"Let's see what Marcia says."

"You better get the hell out of here while you're all whole," said Romano.

Bill put his boot back in the stirrup and glanced up toward the shack he knew Marcia would occupy. He sighed, took another drag on the tattered cigarette and started to move off.

Romano leaped into the trail ahead of him, rifle leveled.

"I'm going to shoot," cried Romano.

Bill leaned over and grabbed the barrel. He canted the rifle and pulled it to him. Romano had to let go or get a broken wrist. Bill jacked the shells out of the magazine and put them into his pocket.

Romano yelled for help and tried to get at his revolver. Bill leaned over and took that and threw it into the brush. With a sharp crack, the rifle butt connected with the seat of Romano's pants.

Bill threw the rifle after the revolver and rode easily up toward the shack.

He got down and walked up the steps. He knocked.

Marcia threw back the door and turned white. She looked hard at Bill and then her eyes began to kindle. Her voice sounded as if words were about to stick in her throat and choke her.

"What do you mean by coming here?" said Marcia, angry.

"Oh, I just thought I'd mosey up and see if you were settled yet," said Bill.

6

"You two-faced, sneaking thief! You . . . you murderer!"

"Well, now," said Bill defensively. "I wouldn't go as far as that. Of course I might have shot Pedro, but . . ."

"Pedro! Another one! First it was Miguel and then Dad and now Pedro. Romano! Romano! Get the men!"

Bill looked at her. He took out a wet handkerchief and mopped at his face. He put it back in his pocket and looked down the trail.

Romano was trying to find the revolver in the brush.

"Get out!" said Marcia, pointing, her mouth set.

Bill looked her over. Yes, he had been right. She was prettier than ever. She was nice and slim and right now she was dressed in a riding skirt and a man's white shirt with rolled-up sleeves. Her brown hair was curly and crisp and feminine. Her face was a perfect oval and her mouth, when she wanted it to be, was kind.

But she could get mad.

"Now look here," protested Bill. "There ain't any use of your getting so up in the air about nothing. I don't know what you're talking about. I knew Miguel got it and that somebody chivvied your dad, but you got the wrong drill bit, Marcia, when you point it at me like that. Shucks, I've been over there at my place sitting around and wishing . . ."

"That won't do you any good," said Marcia in a threatening monotone. "You can't lie out of it now. You should have thought about me before. But it's too late. Too late! Now get out."

"I don't see how anybody can get so doggoned upset about

7

nothing," said Bill. "Course I know that old coyote . . . I mean I know your dad got his in a peculiar way, but what would I be wanting to kill him for?"

"To get this property!" cried Marcia. "You wanted to get all this land, and you aren't content with some of the best drilling ground in this region. You have to have this too and you . . ."

Bill put his hand on her shoulder. He shoved her back into the shack. She tried to fight him, but he shoved her again.

Bill closed the door and bolted it.

A revolver bullet splintered wood about three inches from where his head had been a moment before.

"Romano found his gun," said Bill.

"I hope he did. I . . . I hope he kills you with it."

"Sure now, Marcia, you ain't going to think anything like that. Shucks, Marcia, you and me are old . . ."

"We might have been and I'm sorry for it. You're a great big hulking killer. You're a savage heartless beast! I'm sorry I ever looked at you or saw you. That's it, go on and hit me. Go on and hit me. Romano and my men will be up here in about two minutes and we'll see what happens then."

"Well," said Bill, thoughtfully, "I can't guarantee what happens in the next two minutes, but I sure as hell can guess at what would happen tomorrow."

Frightened, she backed away from him.

Bill sat down in a rocking chair and opened a box of Stewart's cigars. He bit off the end and lighted up with a dry match from the table.

"My men," said Bill, puffing slowly, "would probably come over here and crucify Romano and forget to bury him."

Marcia backed up against the table and looked at him. Her wrath had flared again and the words came in a tumbling flow.

"Your men and you," said Marcia, disdainfully. "A pack of thieves and cutthroats, every one, led by a backwoods roughneck from Arkansas. . . ."

"Texas," corrected Bill.

"You think you can throw this camp into a panic. You think because you bested my dad you've got me licked. Well, you haven't. You haven't! I'm going to see this thing through. I'm going to beat you at your own game if I have to die to do it. I'm going to use your own despicable tools and I'm going to keep on until neither you nor your men are alive."

"Sounds like a threat," said Bill, some of the calm gone from his bearing.

"That's right. You think you can swashbuckle around here because there's no law this far south. You think you can take matters into your own hands and use the powers of life and death. . . ."

"I wouldn't emulate your old man for a million," said Bill, clamping down upon the cigar very hard.

"That's it, malign a man after he's dead. You're rotten. You have no respect for anything. He can't come back here. . . ."

"No, thank God . . . or the devil."

Marcia advanced across the room as though she wanted to strike him. Bill sat right where he was until she was within three feet of him. He stood up and took hold of her shoulders.

Deliberately, he shook her.

"You little wildcat. Come to your senses and act decent, hear me? By God, I ought to turn you over my knee and lick you. You know I didn't do anything to your old man, even though I did hate . . ."

"There!" cried Marcia, stumbling back and panting, throwing her hair out of her eyes with a toss of her head. "There. You see, you admit it. You admit that you hated him and that you killed him . . ."

Bill doubled up his fist and looked at the point of her beautiful chin.

Men were yelling outside. Bill went to the door and opened it. He turned his back on Marcia. She looked eagerly at the wall where a .30-30 hung on pegs.

Bill stepped to the porch. Romano was there, shouting.

"Shoot him!" bawled Romano, well in the rear.

Bill walked down the steps and took the reins of his horse. He turned his back upon the men and started to mount. A big driller named O'Brien lifted a club and struck.

Bill staggered a little. But he managed to swing over the saddle. He jabbed his spurs into the mount's flanks and jerked on the reins.

The pony's hoofs hammered empty air. Bill yanked the horse up on its hind legs and turned it. Indians and drillers scattered.

Several shots rapped close to Bill's head.

He jabbed his spurs again and headed for the edge of the jungle.

Marcia was standing in the doorway crying, holding the

.30-30 in shaking hands. Her head was down and her tousled hair was rumpled from Bill's treatment of her.

But she hadn't shot him.

No. Her finger was on the trigger and she hadn't shot him.

She told herself over and over that you can't shoot a man in the back.

She believed that, did Marcia.

CHAPTER TWO

Arrested for Murder

SOMEBODY told Dad Lacey that nobody ought to wear long underwear in the tropics. Dad Lacey wore long underwear after that.

But he didn't wear a shirt. He saved that for state occasions. Instead he left the sleeves in the red flannels and used safety pins in place of two buttons which had come off sometime in the dim past.

He might have used a bath—in fact it was said that he could have used one for years without soiling it at all. His long mustaches drooped with the sadness of inattention.

But nothing was wrong with his two old Navy Colts. He wore them hung low on either hip and their ivory butts shone with constant care. The barrels looked like twin diamonds when you squinted along them. He even polished the cartridges. His pants contrasted sadly with the gun. They were the color of the jungle mud.

Dad Lacey got up from the bench alongside the main shack of Camp Chico, expectorated very carefully at the Chinese cook's favorite cat and eyed Bill Murphy.

Bill came up and climbed down. He had a welt over his eye and his shirt was torn. He had a hole in his sun hat and his hand was barked.

Bill looked very happy.

"You been in a fight?" asked Dad, somewhat unnecessarily.

Bill went into the shack and sat down. Ching the Chinese brought him a mug of coffee without asking about it. Bill stirred the coffee round and round and slopped it all over the board.

"Women and oil," said Dad, "don't mix."

Bill drank his coffee without noticing that it scalded him. His big hand almost hid the cup as he held it there, empty before his face.

"Them Stewarts," said Dad, "never was much account anyhow."

Bill took a refill and drank that.

"That Marcia is a no-account spitfire. She's puttin' on Northern ways, Bill, and they won't go. You're sure well off without her. I always told you not to mess with them Stewarts. They're pizen. Especially that Mar . . ."

But Dad had ducked in time and the coffee cup missed him by a good inch.

Bill took another cup from Ching, set it down and started to build a smoke.

In a conversational tone of voice, Bill said, "I'll shoot your brains all over the porch for the buzzards to scoop up, if you open your trap again."

Dad Lacey solaced himself with a martyred sigh. "What's wrong, Bill?"

"I been playin' tag with every hunkie in Camp Jaguar. It's lots of fun."

"She turn you down?"

Bill rubbed a match in his hair to dry it and then lighted his smoke. He stretched out his legs and looked squarely at Dad. "Did you kill old man Stewart?"

"That son . . ."

"Be careful," said Bill. "Ching's trying to learn English."

"No, I didn't kill him."

"Who did?" said Bill.

"Damned if I know. Whoever did sure did the country a favor. That old . . ."

"Careful."

"That . . . well, that . . ." Dad coughed, unable to think of a complimentary word. "Anyway, I don't care who chivvied him. Some Injun, I guess."

"Marcia don't think so."

Dad sat up and blinked.

"Marcia says I did it."

"Well for . . . Well, did you ever . . . For God's sake, Bill, is she batty? What would you want to kill old Stewart for? And with a knife, too. That's the part that don't hang, Bill. We've got her there. You ain't any good with a knife. Remember that greaser up in Sonora you tried . . ."

"Forget it," said Bill. "Somebody killed their clerk Miguel and then somebody chivvied Stewart and now Marcia says I did it."

"She ain't in her right senses," yowled Dad. "She ought to be ashamed of herself, accusin' you of usin' a knife like that."

"No, wait," said Bill. "If I killed her dad, then she's plenty sore about it. She thinks I want her land because of this new government order about concession improvement."

"You mean that thing about proving-in a well within two months? Well, we got thirty days left and we've got number three down to seep. She's got hers already proved. What's that got to do with it?"

"She thinks," said Bill, "that we're bluffing it through, that our concession is about wrecked and that I'm trying to save my neck by taking over Camp Jaguar."

"She thinks . . ." began Dad. "Well for gawd's sake."

"And I had to fight my way in and out. They had an Indian ready to bushwhack me and then Romano had left orders for his machine-gun crew to blast me if I showed up, but the guard was asleep. Marcia bawled me out for everything she could think of."

Dad spluttered about that, but Bill didn't notice. Bill was thinking it over again. A smile was on Bill's big face.

"She's sure pretty when she gets mad," said Bill, drawling thoughtfully.

Dad exploded about that. "So they ganged you, did they? So they want a fight, do they? Well, I ain't in love and by God I can talk good and loud when I start."

Dad stomped to the door and took out his guns. He spun them about his index fingers, sent a shot ricocheting between the legs of one of Ching's best cats and swore luridly just as though he had intended to hit it all the time.

Two or three men off shift drifted over to see who had gotten shot. Dad acquainted them with the trouble. More men came and very soon Dad looked like a Communist on

Union Square—with the exception that only his shirt was red, and with a somewhat different locale to back him.

The men stood in the blazing sun and muttered about it but anybody with half an eye could see that they thought a fight would be fine. They were a tough, hard-eyed breed peculiar to the land of derricks—drifters, most of them, fighters all of them by the sheer process of elimination.

There might not be much law in Venezuela, but there were plenty of guns. The men wanted to move off instantly.

A cry from the machine-gun tower stopped them. The man up there yelled, "Here comes somebody. Hey, here comes a whole bunch of guys. Hey, Bill, when do I start squirting lead?"

"Right away," yelled Dad Lacey.

Bill tumbled out of the shack and stared down the trail. "Wait a minute," he ordered the gunner. "Wait a minute, I think that's cavalry."

They couldn't see through the interlacing trees and brush but Bill had caught the glint of sun on metal and he knew that the Camp Jaguar men wouldn't come shined up if they wanted a battle.

Bill stalked down the trail to meet the callers. Behind him his men waited expectantly. Several automatics appeared magically and Dad was seen to lean upon a rifle with great unconcern.

The men coming up the trail were soldiers in the so-called republican army of Venezuela. They were, for the most part, *llaneros* and they looked very smart even after a long ride through the jungle and mud.

In their lead was an officer as slick and smooth and courteous as a Spanish grandee. You could see your face in his boots and his saber chain was gold.

He pulled in when he saw Bill. "*¿Señor, donde esta el chico?*"

"*Aquí mismo,*" said Bill. "Right here."

Two troopers rode easily up as though to hear better.

"*¿Y el señor* Murphy?"

"I am *señor* Murphy."

"*Ya lo creo,*" said the officer. He turned in his saddle and held up his hand.

An instant later the two troopers were close beside Bill and a forest of carbines were covering him.

"*Señor* Murphy," said the officer, "I am *lugarteniente* Herrero. For several days I have had orders for your arrest, but it is so far. I am desolated that I couldn't have come sooner."

"Quite all right," said Bill, rolling himself a smoke. "No inconvenience at all. By the way, *lugarteniente,* what am I arrested for?"

"Oh," said Herrero airily. "Some little thing. Let me see . . . I had the orders. . . . Ah yes, here they are. It says here that you are the murderer of some fellow named . . . named Stewart. Yes, that's it. You're arrested for murdering Stewart."

Bill lit up and leaned on a trooper's saddle. "Is that so?"

"Yes, I suppose it is. See here. There are the orders right there. See, it says Murphy there and Stewart there. Or maybe it's Stewart for murdering. . . . No, that's right. If you'd been murdered, you wouldn't be here, would you?" Herrero thought that that was a pretty fair joke and he smiled, his teeth spectacular against his olive skin and dark mouth.

"I suppose you'll want to take me to Maracaibo, won't you?"

"I suppose so, *señor*. Long ride, eh? And a dry one too. I'm sure the judges wouldn't have sent us if it hadn't been very, very bad. Bah, what's one man more or less up here, eh?"

"Who signed the order?" said Bill.

The *lugarteniente* inspected his orders again. "Ah, some *señorita*, I see. Ah, yes, the *señorita*, the daughter of this Stewart. Hmm, I think I have seen her in Maracaibo. So white with eyes so blue and with such a figure. *Por Dios*, it would be a pleasure to be so charged by that girl. Ah, well, it's a long ride. You have a horse? It would be a pity to walk."

Bill looked back at his drillers. They were no match for thirty troopers well armed, and the machine gun, because Bill was in the road, would be useless.

"Dad," Bill shouted back, "Dad, bring me a horse."

Dad Lacey presently came down to them, scowling and leading Bill's fresh mount.

"What's the charge, Herrero?" said Dad, gruffly, palms itching to get at the two Colts.

"Oh, murder, I think, or some such small thing. But I do not think we will shoot this pleasant *señor* Murphy. That would be quite a shame, you know. Maybe he will get off."

"Look here," said Dad, "when does the trial come up?"

"The court convenes in *octubre*," said Herrero.

"Four months!"

"Yes, about that."

"Why, you white-livered . . ."

"Dad!" said Bill. "Maybe the *lugarteniente* is learning to talk English."

19

"Look here," said Dad, excitedly. "We've only got thirty days to bring this well in and if you keep Bill for four months, we'll lose this concession right off. That's no way to do. Let him bring that well in first and then come and arrest him."

"I am sooooo sorreee," said Herrero.

Bill climbed his horse. "So long, Dad," he said with a wink.

Dad growled and stamped and swore some more and then Herrero turned in the trail and followed it back toward Maracaibo. Bill rode with one heel hooked in the right stirrup, slouched and unworried. He was rolling a smoke when Dad last laid eyes on him.

CHAPTER THREE

In a Dingy Cell

A Venezuelan *cárcel* is a very bad place. Most good Venezuelans appreciate company very much and for that reason a small thing like a sulfur candle is practically taboo.

Consequently, Bill Murphy was not lonesome. He had a jolly crew of bedbugs and some others not quite big enough to see and as though this were not enough, the guards had put him in with a gentleman known as *el Opio*, so called because of a peculiar taste for that drug.

On first inspection, the cell appeared to hold forth no interest whatever, but when the guards had clanged the cell door behind Bill, what appeared to be a pile of sacks reared up and said, "I am twenty-five feet tall and I need one hundred *bolívars*."

Bill blinked in the musty, sweaty gloom and saw *el Opio*. The man was very thin and had a leaden pallor. His eyes were pinpoints and his face twitched a little. His nose was as startling as a parrot's beak.

"I am fifty feet tall," said *el Opio* with great conviction, "and I could snap you in two with one bite if I wanted."

Bill leaned cautiously against the wall and regarded his cellmate.

"How long are you in for?"

"In where?" said *el Opio*.

21

"In here," said Bill.

"Oh, so you're surprised to see me in the palace, eh? Well, they made me dictator yesterday and I haven't quite gotten used to it. They forgot to bring me my clothes. By the way, *señor*, you better give me thirty *bolívars* before I have you shot."

"I have no money," said Bill.

"Neither have I," said *el Opio,* practically. "That's why I want some." Discouraged, he melted into the pile of sacks again and was presently snoring.

Bill looked out of the small window into the pitch-black night and wondered where Marcia was. She certainly was acting funny, the little wildcat. No money was right. If he had to stay in here for four months he'd be a broken-down oil bum, completely penniless. His concession would be gone. It was unlikely that the men could prove it up and bring in oil without him there. Besides, Camp Jaguar seemed to mean business and he guessed they would stop at very little to gain their end.

Footsteps rapped upon the stones in the corridor. Herrero stuck his head in the door opening and smiled, only a set of teeth in the gloom.

"As I was leaving," said Herrero, "I saw a friend of yours that wanted to see you."

Bill didn't care anything about being seen in here with *el Opio* snoring over against the wall and with these brown racers dashing madly upon their various ghoulish businesses.

"Who?"

"This soooo beautiful lady, *la señorita* Stewart."

Bill felt as though Herrero had shot him. He gulped and

said, "Show her in, you worm-faced yap. Show her in. Don't stand there and . . ."

As this was all in English, Herrero failed, luckily, to catch the drift of it. He gathered, however, that the *señorita* was to be shown in and he went away to accomplish that mission as a bold and dashing officer should.

Bill heard them coming down the corridor. Herrero was talking somewhat loftily about how a place of this sort irked a man who was used to the castles of the upcountry, but that the castles irked one too if they were empty of fair ladies. Herrero added, with great grace and poise, that the *señorita* was probably the most beautiful woman in the world and that it would be something of a pleasure to suffer the most exquisite agonies on her behalf.

Through all this, although he did not hear Marcia say a single word, Bill was gradually getting mad. It took quite a while to get men mad where Bill came from. It usually had fatal consequences.

And when Marcia arrived at the cell and though Bill was really mad at Herrero, she received the full force of Bill's anger.

"So you've come down here to gloat about it," snarled Bill between the door bars.

"I understand that you gave up without a struggle," said Marcia, standing there in the gloom, switching at her short boots with a riding crop. "I always knew you were a coward and that proves it. You're where you belong now. Tomorrow I'll see to it that the judges get the evidence the way I got it."

Herrero stepped back a little, awed by the volley of fast words. He knew nothing of their meaning as they were said

23

in English, but he could not mistake the tone. This woman, thought Herrero, was a woman who could hate!

"It's a swell plan," said Bill. "A swell plan. You trump up this murder business and then have me held for trial until my concession option expires and then you take it out and have me shot or pitched on the beach without a cent. Don't talk to me about being a sniveling yellow pup. Don't talk to me about murder. You're worse than your old man!"

And that was about as high as Bill could go.

But Marcia could do a little better than that. When love apparently turns to hate, some perverse demon takes hold of people which makes them want to hurt the former object of affection more cruelly than any Spanish Inquisition. Perhaps it is a wish to justify such an unreasonable emotion.

"To think that I ever let you make love to me. To think that I believed all those things you told me down here two years ago. I thought you were fine and brave. I thought you were the kind of a man who at least had the courage to fight fair. And what are you? What are you? A rotten hulk, worse than a *jacaré*. Well, if this stay in jail loses you your concession, you ought to lose it. This country has been wrecked by guttersnipes like you and it's better off without them."

Bill glared at her. "You cooked all this up. You thought it all out. You know that the lake under Camp Jaguar is an extension of the one under my property. You know that you wouldn't get any oil if I started to cut off the pressure. You're pretty smart—for a girl. Pretty smart."

She moved closer to him and Bill tried to get one hand out as though he wanted to throttle her.

24

Herrero suddenly exploded into action. He cracked his whip across Bill's face and even in the darkness it was possible to see the ugly welt.

Marcia whirled about. Her own riding crop smacked against Herrero's cheek.

"You beast!" cried Marcia. "How dare you strike a defenseless man!"

Herrero was very puzzled and wounded as he fell back. He left the field to Marcia and Bill.

Bill grinned suddenly, but Marcia's face was a beautiful marble mask. She turned and left him.

Bill sat down and *el Opio* sat up and said, "I am fifty-five feet high and I could carve out your heart with one fingernail. Have you got ten *bolívars*?"

Bill turned and you couldn't follow the course of his fist. Fifty-five feet of terror folded up and went to sleep.

Something was scratching just outside the window. Bill sat up and wondered if they were going to murder him where he was, right there in that rotten cell.

The scratching grew louder.

*Marcia whirled about. Her own riding crop
smacked against Herrero's cheek.*

CHAPTER FOUR

Dad Lacey Leads the Way

IT was Dad Lacey's voice.

"Hey, Bill," he said hoarsely. "You in there?"

Bill went to the window. "Get out of here, you old fool. There's a cavalry squadron stationed within a block of here and the whole jail is filled with soldiers and cops."

"Humph, what do I care about that? You put yourself into it today. Why didn't you let them come up to the shack and get you, huh? When you went down to meet them, we couldn't cut loose. Don't you do anything like that again."

"I'm not likely to," said Bill, thinking about the trial.

"Hey, you hunky," rasped Dad Lacey to someone under him. "Quit wiggling around. You'll upset me."

Bill saw then that Dad stood upon the knees of a rider under him. The old man was far from agile when he saw hard work in sight, but here he was, like an acrobat.

"You just sit still," said Dad. "We'll spring you in about fifteen seconds."

His head disappeared and a horse snorted outside. Saddle leather creaked and Bill realized that the whole gang had come down to meet him and get him out. He felt much better about that.

Presently the sound of voices, very excited, came from the orderly room, immediately followed by an explosion.

Boots thundered down the hallway and Dad appeared on the other side of the door jangling a set of keys. He unfastened the lock and Bill strode out.

"Come on," said Dad, "there's a whole passel of cavalry coming."

They ran down the corridor to the guard room. Two drillers were there with drawn guns, staring at the street. Bill stepped over a badly battered and securely handcuffed guard captain and went through the door.

The rest of the men were there, mounted and waiting for him. They had his horse which they had gotten in some mysterious fashion from the cavalry stables.

Bill swung up.

A bugle was blaring on the edge of the lake. A rider tumbled out of a side street and thundered up to Dad. "They're on their way."

"Let's go," said Dad.

They rolled out of the narrow streets of Maracaibo like an avalanche. They were yelling and applying a liberal whip.

Behind them a body of closely packed troopers made the cobblestones ring and the asphalt sing with their swift passage.

On a street corner three shadows ran out, carrying a longer, darker shadow. The latter began to fire with long, lethal streams of flame.

The machine-gun bullets cracked above the heads of the mounted men.

"Ride!" yelled Dad with great vigor.

The command could not have been heard above the yammer

of guns and the roar of hoofs, and it was already being obeyed with the greatest of alacrity.

Bill's men were stringing out, the better to throw off pursuing fire. The better mounted cavalry was catching up with them when they reached the flat outskirts of the town.

For a matter of minutes, capture and annihilation looked certain and then the genius of Dad came forth in a burst of glory.

The Camp Chico machine gun was planted at the crossroads under the command of a man named Edwards. The first group lashed by without a pause and then the cavalry curved into sight.

There was just enough moon to show up their glinting metal.

The machine gun began to chatter.

With one accord the troopers yanked rein and went about on another tack. They scattered in every direction, taken completely by surprise.

When they discovered where the machine gun had been planted and how they could get around it, the gun was gone and the crew was gone and Bill and his men were far up the trail toward Camp Chico.

They eased off after a while, doubting that the troopers had any stomach for more surprises. Bill rode with some of his old slouch and Dad grew conversational.

"Didn't want to kill any of them," said Dad. "No use getting them mad, I guess."

"'Course not," said Bill. "That was pretty well planned."

"Darned if it wasn't," said Dad. "After this we'll double

the camp guard and make certain that nothing gets within a mile of us. Hell, man, we've got to bring in that well or starve."

"I sure wish I knew how I could square myself over at Camp Jaguar," said Bill. "I seem to be in bad all around. By the way, Dad, did you leave anybody to guard the well?"

Dad looked startled. He gulped and looked around. He had taken the machine gun and all the men had followed him.

"Damn you, O'Malley!" Dad roared at a big shouldered giant riding on his left. "I told you to stay back there and here you are. . . ."

"The hell you did," said O'Malley, shifting a chew.

Dad, failing there, tried to find some other target for the blame, but Bill was staring at him in a peculiar way and Dad thought it prudent to shut up.

They quickened their pace after that. They all had a sinking sensation that something would happen to that well during their absence. And if something happened to Camp Chico, they would be a lot of bums on the beach. They were already thinking up ways and means of bumming a ride back to the States before an hour was up.

Bill sighed deeply every now and then as though he had more than a man could bear upon his shoulders. Too bad about that little wildcat. Gee, they used to have such a swell time too. Once out on the lake they'd almost drowned in a sudden squall and she had clung to him and whimpered with terror and when he had set her safely ashore, she had let him kiss her. That had been the first time Bill really found out what love was.

Thinking about past beauties, Bill became very discouraged. Marcia would never look at him again. For a moment he considered going off someplace and drinking himself to death and then, with characteristic buoyancy, he thought about the way she had hit Herrero for hitting Bill. That was something that way. Maybe she didn't hate him, but only thought she did.

Bill had heard something about people doing all manner of crazy things when they were in love. Maybe that was one of them. Maybe she wanted to believe in him after all and had a big fight on her hands to keep hating him. Maybe that was it.

As for the camp, she wouldn't try anything there. She wasn't that bad. Not Marcia. She wouldn't fight in the dark without showing her colors.

Bill had cheered up immeasurably when they came down the last kilometer to Camp Chico.

And then the storm was upon them.

"Who's that?" cried a man named Hathaway, up front.

The challenge was answered with a blasting roar and Hathaway pitched out of his saddle into the muck of the trail.

Instantly guns began to bang.

Through the bedlam, Bill heard a harsh, commanding voice. Romano was there with his unholy crew.

Romano was trying to destroy the well.

CHAPTER FIVE

Out of Jail—Into War

"THEY'LL get at the well," yelled Bill. "Stop the so-and-sos!"

It was instantly apparent that this would be a hard task. Romano was there with almost a hundred whites and Indians and each and every one of them brandished some sort of a weapon.

More than that, Romano and his men were between the Camp Chico outfit and the well. Somewhere in the jungle, Romano's guides were thrashing about trying to flank the riders and somewhere ahead, Romano was shouting:

"Mount that gun, *tonto*! Mount that gun and give it to them, you idiots. Clear them off the trail."

The Camp Chico gun was coming up under Edwards. In this country where bandit attacks were no uncommon thing—the country being so far removed from the spheres of law and order (what there was of it in Venezuela)—machine guns were quite as common as rain.

Bill, however, had the slight advantage of knowing the terrain around his own camp. Whipping up his weary horse, he darted off to the right.

Before him, outlined by a sliver of moonlight, a guide reared up with an ugly machete and tried to reach the saddle.

Bill drew and shot from the hip. The man staggered back into the brush, either dead or seriously wounded.

Bill held his revolver up about the level of his head and rode hard through the thick tangle. Behind him a machine gun began to chatter and Bill wondered whether it was his own. If Romano succeeded in bringing his into action, then the trail would be cleared in a matter of seconds and Bill would have to find himself another crew.

He was going blindly now, lost in the dark, beyond the spreading flanks of Romano's rabble. He had only one thought in mind. He had to get between Romano and the well. That done, things would take care of themselves, or of Bill.

It did not enter his head that he was about to challenge the whole opposing force by himself. Bill was a big fellow, weighing about two hundred pounds and all of it hard muscle and bone, but he was not bulletproof, even though, riding here in the sweltering blackness, he felt like a whole regiment of cavalry.

"Damn little wildcat," muttered Bill, admiringly.

The fact that anyone would fight him did not annoy Bill. Before him, his father had been an oilman of the hard-fighting school. Bill had been raised in boom camps through Texas and Oklahoma and although he had deserted that part of the world for the tropics, he still retained a Texan's ideas of a good time. A swell fight.

Coming about again he charged in toward the clearing where his shacks were. If Dad Lacey was careful he would not force Romano into the advantageous position of the camp. That was made to defend and it would cost men to retake it. But if Romano were still out there on the trail, the task would be a simple one—so thought Bill.

He spotted a flare ahead. That would mean an enemy group. The machine gun became louder and louder. Then it *was* Romano's gun. Maybe the trail and the men had been swept beyond help.

The stabbing orange flames looked like a bloody lance in the darkness. Bill was coming up broadside to it.

Three Indians and a white man were squatted around the gun, feeding in a long belt into the weapon. Clinking, bright metal empties spewed from the breach in a yellow stream. The faces in half-light had a diabolical look as they bent over the gun and the sights.

The Indian who fired was hunched over, legs reaching far out on either side of the gun. His sharply featured face was drawn into a twisted snarl as he compressed the trigger.

Bill broke from the jungle like the squadron he thought he was. The revolver in his hand canted down and jumped up again.

The man on the trigger turned half around in his seat and stayed that way for an instant. Then, as though something had ripped the backbone out of him, he pitched forward.

The torch lighted up the other faces. The white man came up on his knees staring, hands turned to stone on the belt. The other two Indians leaped up and snatched at machetes.

Bill slapped down with the revolver. His horse was rearing and he missed. The white man grabbed the gun and swiveled it around.

With a chopping motion, Bill jabbed a streak of flame at

35

him. The gun muzzle tipped abruptly up and shot a short burst straight at the slivered moon.

The other two took to their heels. Men were yelling in the jungle. A wave of shadows ran like ink out of the brush and came down upon the machine gun.

Bill could neither run nor stay. He did not dare turn his back upon this rushing horde. And he could not face those singing, yowling slugs which ripped up the air about his head.

The horse between his legs screamed. Bill felt his mount going. He leaped aside and out of the saddle before the stirrups touched ground. The horse tried to lift its head again and fell back.

The tide of shadows was close now. The flare of exploding powder lit up the clearing. Bill started up and looked hastily behind him.

He suddenly felt small and weak and vulnerable. Any one of these buzzing bullets could cut him down forever. But he had to stay there and take it. He was about to drop under the protection of the dead horse and he caught sight of the machine gun again.

That had been his main objective. He leaped for it now. With rough hands he threw the white man and the Indian away from it. A half-length was in the breech, waiting to go.

Bill let them have it. The chattering, jumping weapon pumped five hundred slugs in a half circle in less than a minute. The blaze fanned out, spreading orange light over the ground, lighting up the faces of the charging men.

Suddenly they realized what they faced. Three of them dropped in the lead. The rest of them turned and sprinted for the jungle. In a moment they would have snipers from two angles on the job.

Bill looked around again. He threw a coil of belts over his arm and scooped up the gun, scorching his fingers. Heavily he loped toward the machine-gun tower. That, at least, had sandbags around the top as a protection from bullets. It was built of steel and could not be fired from the ground.

Climbing the ladder was something else.

A rung disappeared an instant before Bill put his hand on it. He heard the sharp scream of the maimed slug going away. Snipers along the jungle edge were trying to shoot him off that long, long ladder.

The tower itself was about seventy-five feet high. It reared up its skeleton against the thin mist of the moon, a shaky, tall thing which shivered every time Bill put down a foot.

He had to climb with one hand, holding the gun with the other. It was no small feat. He had to let go his hold for a split second to grab the next each time he moved up. For that split second he was sagging back over the ground and if, in the darkness, he missed one grip, he would hurtle down to destruction.

His helmet sailed away from his head, almost tearing his chin off when the strap refused to go.

They had him now. He was a smoky silhouette against the moon, an excellent target. The slugs began to whine closer and closer. They were getting the range and he could not move fast enough to throw them off their sights.

"Damn that little wildcat," said Bill, hitching upward an inch at a time.

37

The top looked far, far away, unattainable as the moon above it. Even a wounding bullet would kill him by knocking him loose.

"Damn that Dad Lacey anyhow," said Bill. "But he did get me out of jail."

He began to think about that time that it was far better to be listening to *el Opio* grow taller and taller than to be here climbing to the very moon, weighted down with a gun and tripod which, in usual warfare, were meant to be carried by two men along level ground.

The shooting quickened in the jungle. Bill knew that it was all up. He could never get to the top. Never. He would climb up another rung and then a leaden fist would crack him down and he would pitch earthward to a bone-cracking jolt and death.

He had seen Edwards go up this tower every morning for months. Edwards would go up like a cat, faster than you could follow him, just as though he had wings.

Again the firing quickened below.

Bill glanced at the jungle and saw that a number of streaks were at right angles to him.

"Get 'em, Dad," yowled Bill. "Get the sons!"

With another whoop of joy, Bill went on up the tower, undisturbed by bullets. Good old Dad. He wasn't so dumb after all. He had led a very clever flanking movement to the left and now he and his men were covering Bill's ascent up the tower. Of course Dad could not long hold his position. He would have to fall back in a matter of seconds.

Bill's fingers reached out and grabbed the platform edge.

He boosted up the heavy gun which weighed three and a half tons by this time—and shoved it to safety behind the sandbags.

With an upward swing, Bill heaved himself over the top and hunched down behind the protecting barrier.

Hastily he set up the gun, loaded it and began to look for targets.

He had been right about Dad's position. Dad was lying down there in the jungle, almost surrounded. The question was, where was Dad and where was Romano? All flashes looked alike from up against the moon.

Bill saw men scuttling toward the shacks. Were they his own or were they Camp Jaguar people?

"Bill!" came a thin cry from the jungle. "Bill! Get those damned hunkies out of that shack!"

Dad's voice was instantly drowned by rifle fire, but Bill had the score now. Dad was to the left and Romano was to the right. Somehow they had gotten scrambled up and had swapped positions. Those men who had now begun to blast at the jungle from the shacks were Romano's men.

Bill played the Anvil Chorus on the trigger. The jarring, smoking machine gun belched scorching metal down into the thin boards of the maintenance office.

"It'll leak," said Bill, "when it rains."

He spread a few bursts around to the other shacks and then opened up again on the office.

"I'll have to get tin," said Bill, "and patch the thing up."

A man sprinted out of the door and Bill almost fired at him.

It was Ching, the Chinese cook, closely followed by no less than four frightened cats. Bill covered the man's retreat by a liberal battering of the shack and jungle. Ching disappeared into the darkness beyond.

"I guess," said Bill, "that I'll have to get another cook."

The tower shuddered and Bill raised up to peer over the edge. Two men were coming up, their eyes flashing white when they lifted their heads. They were carrying machetes in their teeth so that their hands would be free as they climbed.

"Damned fools," said Bill.

He picked up a sandbag and held it over the top. He sighted carefully. The men below hastily tried to slide down again. Bill dropped the bomb and drove the pair halfway through to Siberia.

When he came back to the gun again, he saw that the flashes were increasing on the left. Men were trying to clear the tower with hopeful shots.

Bill let them have a couple bursts, and then looked down again. No one else wanted a crack at climbing the tower.

The machine gun leaped like a startled horse. Water gurgled for a moment. A stray slug had split the cooling jacket and the gun was about as useful as a broomstick.

Bill had a funny feeling in the pit of his stomach. He reached for his revolver and couldn't find it. He had dropped it when he dived for the gun.

Well, he had sandbags and as long as they held out . . .

Spaaaaaang!

The slug ripped a long furrow in the platform.

"What the hell . . ." began Bill, crouching behind the bags. That slug had come from either above or the same level.

Peering out between two bags he spotted a shadow on top

of the well derrick. One of Romano's men was trying to finish him off.

Bill's hands itched for a gun. He tried to fire the ruined machine gun and it promptly jammed, forever out of commission.

His position was suddenly very hot. He couldn't lie there and take it. Sooner or later the man on the derrick would nail him.

He couldn't very well climb down and rush across the clearing, but that would be better than lying here making a motionless target.

No sooner said than done, Bill went over the edge of the platform. He slid to the ground so fast that his hands were burned by friction.

He lunged for the jungle, hoping he had the right direction. The ground began to explode under his flying feet. Every rifle along the edge was trying for him, but they had not had enough warning and they were not quite sure that this was another man and that Bill still held down the tower.

He made the edge and dived down, hoping to reach Dad Lacey and the gang. He had not watched this jungle fight as closely as he should have and once down, it was hard for him to know which direction he should take.

He burst into a thicket. It was as if he had flushed a covey of quail. Men scattered in every direction, shouting with surprise. They could not tell that Bill was only one man and when they found out, Bill was in the middle of the rat's nest, trying to get his hands on a weapon to defend himself.

A thin, slick-haired man rose out of the shadows and fired

point blank. But Bill had seen the movement and had dived far to one side.

With a swinging tackle, Bill took the man down in a heap and promptly gave the smooth jaw a couple of fast ones just to make sure.

Men were calling shrilly and excitedly all through the black tangle. Bill held on to his man.

Rifles started up in staccato chorus. Bullets carved long splinters from trunks and showered the matted earth with leaves and branches.

Men were running somewhere and another machine gun started into action.

After a moment all was still. For many seconds it stayed that way and then a voice was calling, "Bill! Hey, Bill! They've beat it."

Bill sat on the stomach of his man and waited for the men to come to him. He was taking no chances on walking into another lot of killers.

"This way," said Bill.

Dad Lacey, a smoking gun in each hand, looking like some ogre from another world, came up snorting and muttering.

"Who you got there, Bill?"

"I dunno," said Bill. "Let's see."

Dad holstered his guns after blowing them out and took a chew with exaggerated calm. Then he picked up the captive's feet and Bill took the head and they carted the unconscious fellow out into the light.

"Romano," said Bill, startled.

"Aha," said Dad. "Lemme kill the *jacaré*, Bill. Lemme kill him right now before he gives us the slip, huh?"

"Bring him up to the shack first," said Bill, more for Romano's foggy benefit than for Dad's.

They laid Romano out on the bunk and Romano was very sick. His face was gray and his eyes were wild and his usually polished hair was sadly muddy and mussed.

"Well, well," said Bill, standing back. "You sure make calls when you call. What's the idea?"

"I'm not the one," whined Romano, trying to sit up. "La *señorita* Stewart give me orders and I have to obey. She say to come over here and kill and so I have to come."

"Yeah?" said Bill.

"Sure, she tell me I have to come and I have to get the men and try. But I know what strong, gallant men you . . ."

"Keep it," said Bill.

Edwards and two other men came in.

"Two dead and three to carry," said Edwards, puffing on a crumpled and damp cigarette.

"Okay," said Bill. "Did anything happen to the well?"

His question was answered before it was wholly out of his mouth. A harrowing yell came from the derrick.

"Bill!" a driller was yelling. "Bill! For gawd's sake come out here."

Bill headed for the door and thrust the obstructions aside. He bolted toward that precious well and saw that men were coming toward it from every direction.

The damage was instantly apparent. Machinery had been

43

smashed with a sledge. The walking beam was all out of line and more than that, the drill hole was suspiciously scuffed over.

They went to work immediately and after a half-hour's concentrated work they knew the worst.

Bill stood up and wiped an oily hand across his sweating brow. O'Malley was grieving noisily. Others looked as though they had been hit by a soup wagon.

"There's a wrench down there," said Edwards, at last. "They've wrecked us. If we can't fish it out, we'll have to start another well."

Dad Lacey sighed gustily. "I better go in and kill that Romano," said Dad.

"Romano?" said Edwards. "I thought you were staying there to guard him."

"You didn't do anything of the kind!" roared Dad. "I thought you were. I told you . . .

"The hell you did!" shouted Edwards.

Bill sprinted for the shack and looked inside. It was, as he suspected, quite empty.

"Damn," said Bill, wearily. "It was going too well. I knew it was. And now . . ."

Dad was trying to explain how he had told Edwards to stay behind, but Bill wouldn't listen to him.

"Dad," said Bill, "bear with me yet a while. I'm going down to Maracaibo and pick up a whole new outfit for another well."

"After we spend a whole night getting your carcass out of that jail. . . ."

Bill cut off the wail. "There's only one thing for it. We've got twenty-nine days to hit oil."

"But we can't!" cried O'Malley in the doorway.

"It's impossible!" yelled Dad.

"Wake me up about nine," said Bill, stretching out on his bunk boots and all and getting the blankets muddy. "Now post somebody up in that tower and . . . Oh, yes, send out a party to find Ching and his cats. They're halfway to Brazil by now."

They were about to protest further but Bill, with a smile on his face, was softly snoring, and perhaps dreaming about Marcia Stewart.

CHAPTER SIX

A Joke Proves Dangerous to Bill

BILL MURPHY rode into the outskirts of Maracaibo about four o'clock. He had come by the back trails, avoiding the roads which he knew might be watched.

He had a problem on his hands and a big one. Somehow or other, in spite of Marcia and Romano and the troopers, he had to get a hydraulic rotary drill and he had to transport it by truck, dray or hand, if necessary, back to Camp Chico.

Although Bill, in many instances, had been known to show a remarkable instinct for getting into trouble through sheer bullheadedness, this time he went about the job with a great deal of finesse.

He could not walk into Maracaibo as Bill Murphy, oilman. And so he decided that he would walk in there as Harvey Johnson, tourist.

To this end he directed his steps to a small hut almost lost in a tangle of hot brush. An old man lived there with no visible means of support, but the old man always had a little bit of this and that around the place.

The old man was sitting on his steps, drowsing in the afternoon sun when Bill sighted him.

Bill rode closer and the old man failed to move. Bill swung down off his horse and walked the intervening distance and stared, abruptly, into a drawn .45 automatic.

"Wait a minute," said Bill, drawing it out slowly. "No need to get flighty, Ledeaux."

The old man blinked and then recognized Bill. Sheepishly he pocketed the .45, got up and stretched.

"You ought to be more careful, *señor* Murphy," said Ledeaux. "Never walk up on a man in my circumstances without making some noise. Why, I might have shot you."

Bill grinned at him. Ledeaux, even now, bore some of the stamp of his days in French Guiana from which he had escaped some ten years before. Authorities seldom paid any attention to him, but, as Ledeaux sometimes hinted, three gentlemen he had left behind might someday appear and object to the fact that he had left wearing some of their clothes and carrying most of their cash.

"What can I do for you?" said Ledeaux, mopping his greasy face with his ragged sleeve.

"I want some clothes," said Bill.

"But, *señor*," protested Ledeaux, "why have you come to me? You see that I myself am in rags. How could I have clothes and not wear them?"

Bill grinned again. As Ledeaux was the fence and the head mobster of Maracaibo's petty crime, he had to put up some kind of a front to comparative strangers.

With slow deliberation, Bill took a handful of *bolívars* out of his pocket. He poured them from one hand to the other and back again. Ledeaux watched with greedy fascination, licking his thick lips.

"I want clothes. I want," said Bill, "a disguise. I want to

48

look like a tourist and my name is Harvey Johnson. You, Ledeaux, are pretty good at that sort of thing, you know."

"You flatter me, *señor*," said Ledeaux. "But come. We stand here frying in the sun. Come in and have some coffee with me. And for the sake of the good God, put away that money. Here, I'll take it if you have no pockets."

As they moved through the doorway of the mean hut, a shadow drifted across the compound, unseen by either of them. In a dark place beside the wall, the shadow stopped in a listening attitude.

But Bill watched nothing but Ledeaux. The old man pulled up a trapdoor and lowered himself into a lower room. Presently he thrust a pair of suitcases up and followed them immediately.

The suitcases were stamped with stickers taken from almost anyplace in the world, quite obviously the property of a tourist. Chuckling, Ledeaux unstrapped them and looked inside.

"Where?" said Bill.

"A tourist, so big, gave them to a man he thought was a porter," chuckled Ledeaux.

Bill, although he did not favor dealing with either Ledeaux or stolen goods, had to take what he could get. He nodded affably.

Ledeaux was hauling forth a white suit which looked as though it might fit Bill. He followed it with a *jipijapa* hat which had probably cost the luckless tourist about fifty dollars in Ecuador.

Bill stripped off his muddy khaki and shed his boots. He pulled on the white pants. But Bill was built something like a prize fighter and he had a waist as narrow as his shoulders were wide. Evidently this tourist had faired well on hotel food and when Bill put the suspenders up the belt band billowed and puffed and was somehow twice too big.

But the coat covered that and when Bill had tied the flowing dark tie and had picked up a cane in the corner, he grinned with satisfaction—until he stepped to a mirror. That gave him a shock. He still looked like Bill Murphy.

"Here," said Ledeaux. "I fix that right away. Once I was in the theater business."

"Robbing box offices?" said Bill.

"No. Stealing out of the dressing rooms," corrected Ledeaux with some pride.

The old man produced a makeup kit and took out some line pencils and some gray hair. He snipped away with his shears, daubed some spirit gum on Bill's upper lip and then applied the mustache.

With powder Ledeaux grayed Bill's hair and with the line pencils, he put pouches under Bill's eyes and some wrinkles on Bill's cheeks and forehead.

Bill looked in the mirror again and saw a very kindly old gentleman, probably a southerner.

"Yes, suh," said Bill, giving the *jipijapa* white hat a rakish tug. He spun the cane and admired himself again.

Ledeaux gave him a handful of papers and chuckled. "You look just like him."

"Like who?" said Bill.

"George Henderson, the Standard representative that arrived last week. See, you think I am not good, eh?"

Bill blinked at himself in the mirror. "Don't you think I look sort of flappy around the waist for that?"

Ledeaux promptly produced a small pillow and tucked it into Bill's pants.

A few more *bolívars* changed hands and Bill walked outside into the sun, trying to be as pompous as possible. He did not see the shadow against the wall. The sun was too blinding for that even when a sliver of steel, incredibly sharp, glittered in the unknown's hand.

Bill walked slowly as he neared the main part of town. Nobody looked at him or saluted him and finally he began to feel better.

He was coming into the city through Haticos, the swanky lake residential section south of the main town, and he surveyed the houses as though he owned each and every one.

When he reached the main drag he was more confident than ever, until he spotted two police officers standing in close conference on the corner.

He had to pass them and he swung the cane and approached. Just opposite them, one of the officers reached out and touched his arm. Bill's heart went down into his boots.

"*Señor,*" said the officer, "*¿Es usted el señor Jorge Henderson, verdad?*"

Bill choked. "*Sí, sí.* I am George Henderson."

Bill had to bat his eyes rapidly to keep from betraying himself. Of course he should have thought of this. The Standard representative here in this town had about as much power as the governor himself because he was the reason for Maracaibo's main activity—petroleum. That damned Ledeaux was altogether too clever with his makeup. This expensive *jipijapa* hat and the good quality whites had done the trick. Nobody in Maracaibo wore such things.

"*Bueno,*" said the officer, "we have been watching for you since you have not been at home all morning. We were instructed to warn you, if we saw you, not to make the trip to Camp Jaguar. Things are upset in the back country."

"*Gracias,*" said Bill. "*Muchas gracias, señores,*" and got away from there.

He had food for thought, however. Marcia, then, was playing for a sellout to Standard Petroleum.

He hadn't thought she would do that. He was disappointed in her. Perhaps she was putting up this fight with Standard money behind her. Bill walked more slowly and felt blue. She was selling him out, after all. She wanted Camp Chico only because Standard would not buy Jaguar unless that oil lake, thousands of feet down, was wholly under Jaguar control.

He felt badly in need of a drink and he swung into a big hotel, thinking that was as safe as anywhere. Damn that Ledeaux for making him so conspicuous. But the man had a sense of humor. You couldn't deny that.

Bill stood up to the bar and had a Planter's Punch. As he was sipping it, wondering how he would get that rig, a small native boy came scuttling in. He tugged at Bill's coat with a none-too-clean hand.

"*Señor* Henderson, *¿verdad?*"

"My God," thought Bill, "does everybody in Maracaibo want this Henderson?"

"*Tengo una carta, señor,*" said the boy, holding up a letter.

STORIES from the GOLDEN AGE

☐ Yes, I would like to receive my **FREE CATALOG** featuring all 80 volumes of the *Stories from the Golden Age Collection and more!*

Name
_____

Shipping Address
_____

City _____ State _____ ZIP _____

Telephone _____ E-mail _____

Check other genres you are interested in: ☐ SciFi/Fantasy ☐ Western ☐ Mystery

FREE SHIPPING!
NO PURCHASE REQUIRED

6 Books • 8 Stories
Illustrations • Glossaries

6 Audiobooks • 12 CDs
8 Stories • Full color 40-page booklet

- -
Fold on line and tape

IF YOU ENJOYED READING THIS BOOK, GET THE ACTION/ADVENTURE COLLECTION AND SAVE 25%

BOOK SET	AUDIOBOOK SET
$59.50 $45.00	$77.50 $58.00
ISBN: 978-1-61986-089-6	ISBN: 978-1-61986-090-2

☐ Check here if shipping address is same as billing.

Name
_____

Billing Address
_____

City _____ State _____ ZIP _____

Telephone _____ E-mail _____

Credit/Debit Card #: _____

Card ID # (last 3 or 4 digits): _____

Exp Date: _____/_____ Date (month/day/year): _____/_____/_____

Order Total *(CA and FL residents add sales tax)*: _____

To order online, go to: **www.GoldenAgeStories.com** or call toll-free **1-877-8GALAXY** or 1-323-466-7815

NO POSTAGE
NECESSARY
IF MAILED
IN THE
UNITED STATES

BUSINESS REPLY MAIL
FIRST-CLASS MAIL   PERMIT NO. 75738   LOS ANGELES CA

POSTAGE WILL BE PAID BY ADDRESSEE

GALAXY PRESS
7051 HOLLYWOOD BLVD
LOS ANGELES CA   90028-9771

It was addressed to George Henderson and Bill was about to give it back with some weird excuse when he recognized the handwriting.

Marcia's.

"Gracias," said Bill, slitting open the envelope and giving the boy a coin.

He read: "Mr. Henderson: It has come to my notice that you are attempting to do business about Camp Jaguar. If you wish, I will see you at the *Café de Oro* at eight this evening. Marcia Stewart."

Bill had a little time on his hands until then. He had to get that hydraulic rotary drill. After that he would see Marcia. He would try to bluff it out, if he could. Perhaps she had never met this man. Perhaps, if the lights were dim, she would fail to recognize Bill.

He swung out of the hotel and went down to the waterfront. For a short time he wandered along the twisting quays and then he found the shop for which he searched.

A bright young clerk came to the counter and failed to see anything wrong with his customer.

Bill came to the point. "I want a complete rig and I want it loaded and shipped to Camp Chico by truck tonight. Can you do it?"

"I have a secondhand rotary rig I could let you have."

"Let's see it."

They went into the back of the store and looked over the equipment. Bill was satisfied. He drew a money belt from about his waist and counted a large amount into the clerk's hand.

"The other half is payable on delivery," said Bill. "Have the truck up the trail to Camp Chico. I'll meet the driver there about midnight and go on in with him."

"Will Bill Murphy be around?" said the clerk.

"Well, er, I guess so. I'll have Bill Murphy meet the truck. Your driver know him?"

"Sure. Everybody knows Bill Murphy. He's certainly badly wanted right now. I heard the cops were going to string him up to the nearest lamp post if they spotted him."

"That so?" said Bill. "Well, I guess they'll have to spot him first."

The clerk thought that that was a good joke.

CHAPTER SEVEN

Bill Takes to Flight

THE *Café de Oro,* like all South American *Cafés de Oro,* was fairly respectable. At least it had a front room which was respectable. In the back you could hear the croupier's bored remarks and that peculiar tinkle and rattle which marks the roulette wheel.

Marcia had chosen the place because it was not conspicuous and because, with some amount of precaution, it was not dangerous. She had a small table over against the wall where the lights were dim and, to hide her growing agitation, she was drinking a *limonada* and wishing she had not come at all.

Several *caballeros,* drawn by her beauty, had tried to drum up a conversation with her, but Marcia had proven a little too withering for them.

She was not dressed in an evening gown, as were the other ladies present. She wore a white linen sport ensemble and a big floppy linen hat. She looked all business.

On the stroke of the hour, Bill entered the cafe and looked around. When he saw her he experienced a queer feeling in the region of the heart. He couldn't deceive her. He couldn't, no matter what she had done to him. He turned hastily around and started to leave, but a waiter stopped him.

"*Señor* Henderson. The *señorita* there at that table is waiting to speak with you."

With a weary sigh, Bill went toward her. She did not get up to meet him. In fact, she was not at all kind.

Bill bowed stiffly because of the pillow, removed his hat and sat down. His face was in deep shadow, much to his relief.

"So you," said Marcia, "are George Henderson. The George Henderson, in fact. I rather supposed you would be fat and awkward."

"Hrmph," said Bill.

"It seems, Mr. Henderson, that since my father was killed, I have had nothing but grief. I wish I had never seen Venezuela again. I should have stayed north. I've had several shocks since I have been here and you'll pardon me if I am brief, even abrupt. This business is no more tasteful than the rest."

Bill thought she had very beautiful eyes. He wished she'd be the old Marcia she had been. He wished he had stolen her from old man Stewart when he first saw her.

"Yes," said Bill, gutturally, to encourage her.

"Have you a cold?" said Marcia.

"Fever," growled Bill.

"I should think so," said Marcia. "And I wouldn't be surprised but what you had a higher fever in a few minutes. Mr. Henderson, I think that you greatly desire Camp Jaguar."

"Well, er . . ."

"Of course you do. You've made that very plain. But you do not want Camp Jaguar unless you can have Camp Chico. Right?"

"Well . . ."

"If you want Camp Chico, you will have to deal with Bill Murphy and of course you haven't the courage to do that."

Bill cleared his throat in protest.

"No, you haven't the courage. You're big business. You have the money for anything and you're willing to try anything. I think, Mr. Henderson, that I am beginning to see through a lot of things. Bill Murphy is, of course, a murderer and he has been very unfair in his dealing with Camp Jaguar, but I cannot allow you to use Camp Jaguar as a tool. This is a warning, Mr. Henderson. Hands off upcountry, do you understand? Let oilmen fight this out as they will. Then, if you have enough cash to buy straight over the counter, somebody may sell. But stay away from Jaguar. I am not—and never was—unreasonable. You will find me very fair to deal with. I have been carrying on for my Dad. He might not have been all he should have been, but he would want me to go ahead and finish the work. If, to do that, I must appear hard and unreasonable, then I am. You know what I am talking about, Mr. Henderson. We need not discuss it further."

Bill made some restless movement to get up, but a noise in the street stopped him.

Men were talking excitedly. A car rattled by and men went to the windows to stare at its retreating tail light. Talk buzzed louder and swept into and through the cafe.

A man at the next table said to his partner, "You heard that? But this is terrible! Think what would happen to Maracaibo if Standard . . ."

The girl said, "What was that again. You talk so fast, Jaime."

"Why, don't you hear well? Jorge Henderson, the Standard

representative, was found knifed in the back in the jungle back of town." Jaime, being an oil broker, mopped his brow. "He may even die!"

Marcia Stewart was on her feet staring at Bill, very afraid. Her eyes were big and her hands trembled.

"Then who . . . who are you?" said Marcia.

Bill glanced swiftly about him, looking for an exit. His hand was closed over the revolver he carried in a shoulder holster.

Marcia leaned across the table with sudden courage. She whipped off the mustache and thrust Bill into the light.

"Bill!" she cried, falling back. "Oh. Why did you do it? Why did you have to murder . . . ?"

Bill heard something else. In the street a loud voice bellowed, "Where is this man? It cannot be, I tell you. Where is this man?"

Gun in hand, eyes wild, Herrero, *lugarteniente* of cavalry, lunged into the *Café de Oro* and stared around in confusion.

"It cannot be," panted Herrero, sitting after a hard run. "He was just knifed and it cannot be that he is here. Someone has . . ."

Bill might have shot Herrero in that instant. He did not. Bill lunged for the kitchen at the back and Herrero spotted him.

"There's the . . ." cried Herrero, raising his gun to shoot. His finger came down upon the trigger. He could not miss, even though Bill was going fast.

The gun exploded—and buried a slug in the floor.

Marcia, who had struck the weapon down, stood there and

blocked Herrero as well as she could. She had a small riding crop which she always carried.

She let Herrero have it across the eyes.

"Murderer," she said disdainfully.

Herrero was gone then, off in full pursuit, yelling for his men to follow him.

Pans clattered in the kitchen. A cook screamed. The back door banged once, twice and then the *Café de Oro* stood in paralyzed silence, wondering what had happened and just why. Marcia had somehow disappeared in the street.

CHAPTER EIGHT

Bill Catches a Killer

BILL had very few illusions as to what would happen to him if they caught him. They would naturally think that he had knifed George Henderson so that he could don his disguise without being detected.

That would be enough evidence for Herrero and the courts of Maracaibo. They would make an example out of a man who dared take a punch at that saint among saints, that great religion, Big Business.

And although Bill was pretty sure what had happened, he had no way of proving it.

Somehow he had been spotted in Ledeaux's hut, or maybe they had made Ledeaux talk. His murder had then been ordered.

But in the dark of night, when a white suit and gray mustache were just that and no more, George Henderson had been marked out as being Bill Murphy.

It was, thought Bill, running very hard along an alley, quite a remarkable mixup. He remembered, as he vaulted a wall and rushed through a court, upsetting a table and tripping over a fountain, that Marcia had thought him to be Henderson.

"Shucks!" cried Bill, shying around a corner and knocking over two startled gentlemen in whites. "She ain't in it at all!"

That made him feel so good he almost stopped and waited for the troopers.

A gun barked behind him and plaster came off a wall like snow. Bill took to his heels again, heading for the edge of town.

So Marcia wasn't in it after all. No sir, he had been right all along. There was something more than Marcia's hand in this. Bill prided himself that he had known it all along.

Something about this smelled badly to Bill. Something was up far bigger than either Marcia or himself. He was not sure about anything, but now that he knew he really wasn't fighting that brave young lady he loved so well, he had enough courage to do some attacking on his own.

Funny, thought Bill, to think at all of attacking when you were running as fast as your legs could carry you through a scorching tropical night toward an objective which might or might not prove your undoing.

Attacking was somehow out of the question when a bullet missed you on the average of one every two minutes.

His lungs were bursting when he finally reached the outskirts. He didn't intend to leg it through jungle and he would have to stay off the main roads. Somehow he had to get back his horse and rifle and his own clothes.

Bill turned into an alley and pressed himself against the black shadows under the wall. Feet were hammering up the street he had just left. Men were yelling out to one another and acting like so many beagles on the trail of an exhausted rabbit.

The troopers charged by, sabers clanking, revolvers ready for the execution. Herrero was puffing and blowing but still going strong, his white teeth bared the better to catch his breath.

Bill watched them go and grinned. When they rounded another corner and swept out of sight, he stepped back to the street. The troopers were still chasing him—so they thought.

Bill ran into another alley, crossed a garden, dropping a "Pardon me" as he knocked down the proprietor, vaulted the far wall and ran up another alley.

His course was a crazy zigzag, and although many people marked his progress and sent word that a mysterious Americano was upsetting the better part of Maracaibo, Bill left no trail worth following.

Outside of town the troopers would be watching every road and trail. Bill would have to fight that out as he came to it.

He spotted Ledeaux's mean shack and promptly dashed across the yard and kicked in the door.

Ledeaux stood up with ready gun, out of a sound sleep. When he recognized Bill, Ledeaux grinned.

"Laugh, damn you," said Bill. "You're funny, you are. You know what happened? They knifed Henderson, that's what. And they spotted me after it happened."

Ledeaux let out a frightened squeak. "B-But . . . But . . . My God, get out of here. Get out before . . ."

Bill shucked off the white clothes, recovered his boots and whipcord breeches from the corner and dressed. He girded on a spare gunbelt and picked up a box of shells from Ledeaux's dressing table where they lay in a litter of grease paint, dirty dishes and coffee grounds.

Bill washed his face, clapped his sun helmet on his head and went to the door. The yard was clear.

"You better beat it," said Bill. "They may track me here and want to search the place."

"S-S-Search?" gasped Ledeaux.

"Yeah. Clear out. *Adios,* and thanks for the party."

Bill hauled his pony out of a shed, saddled up, slung the rifle over his shoulder and mounted. Somewhere out there in the blackness he would run across Herrero again. He was sure of that. He hated to have to shoot a trooper. That would put a bad light on things. Maybe they would have some Indian guides with them. If they did, he could shoot one just to show them he meant business.

Darting a glance to the right and left, he dug in his spurs and went up the dark trail at a rapid lope. The houses were not many through this part of town and the people in them were not the least bit curious when they heard a fast horse going in the direction of the hills. In fact, these flat-faced, slow moving people were not the least bit curious of anything. It is reported that a corpse laid between two of these shacks for three days without any inquiry whatever being made about it. The people said, of course, that they didn't know it was there, which, of course, was somewhat away from the truth, knowing what corpses do in the tropic sun.

This night, however, was an exception, but if it had not been, Bill would have loped on by without noticing.

A man was standing just off the trail, a white fuzz in the blackness. He tried to hide when Bill approached and Bill had the sudden premonition that the man had been watching for him.

Bill, although the horse was still churning mud, threw himself off at a run and hauled in on the bridle.

The man detached himself from the palm tree and tried to get away.

For an instant Bill hesitated. The fellow might be some petty thief trying to get out of the city. But why he had been waiting until Bill came, only the shadow could answer. Bill wanted the answer.

He sprinted after the man and made a shallow dive at the flying legs.

Hit by two hundred pounds of hard muscle and bone, the man went down with a thud which made the earth shiver. Bill rolled him over and lit a match.

"*El Opio,*" said Bill, amazed.

"*Señor,*" said *el Opio,* sitting up with some difficulty and feeling of his bones, "*Señor,* you are fortunate. I am not so tall tonight."

"What the hell are you doing here?"

"I was waiting for . . . for . . ."

"A streetcar," said Bill. "When did you get out of jail?"

"You let me out, *señor.*"

"That's unfortunate," said Bill. "You know, *el Opio,* I have a peculiar dislike for you. In fact, I think I'd slit your throat if I had a knife. Have you got one."

"No, no, no."

"Hmm, and guns make such a lot of noise. That's too bad

you haven't a knife. You've got a bad record in Maracaibo. I understand that you do killing for as little as five *bolívars*."

"Twenty!" cried *el Opio*, his professional pride touched to the quick.

"And you didn't collect tonight, did you, *el Opio*? No gow for you, that right?"

"You got some?" he said, eyes shining expectantly, clawlike fingers reaching out.

"No. No, I don't use it, *chico*," said Bill, "and besides, I don't like you. Once I didn't like a guy and you know what I did? I took my bare hands like this. I put them right around his throat and then I began to push in like this. . . ."

"Blug," cried *el Opio*, squirming and prying at Bill's hands.

"And then I let them up like this," said Bill, calmly. "And then I pushed in like this. There's a science to it. When you do this, you block all the blood out of a man's head and he goes out like a light. And then you bring him to and let him breathe for a couple minutes and then . . ."

"¡Señor!" wailed *el Opio*, "Do not do that!" He rubbed his neck ruefully. "You were choking me."

"I'm sorry," said Bill. "I really wasn't choking you. It really hurts when you do it this way. You take the back of the man's neck . . ."

"¡Cristo!"

"*El Opio*, I do not like you very much and I need practice with my choking. Let me take . . ."

"*Señor*, what is it you want? I will talk. I will talk. Truly I will. I . . . I . . . I am not so tall tonight, *señor*."

"Did you kill George Henderson?"

66

"No!"

"Then I shall have to . . ."

"Yes, yes, *señor*. I knifed him, but it wasn't him. I thought that . . ."

"I am afraid," began Bill, "that I shall have to . . ."

"I was supposed to kill you!" wailed *el Opio*. "But I made a mistake. I thought he was you because you looked like him!"

"Fine. You can tell me lots later. Right now we've got to get out of Maracaibo."

Bill picked up *el Opio* (and *el Opio* wasn't a very small man at all) and threw him across the saddle. Then Bill strapped down his hands and feet and tied them together under the horse's belly and they went on up the trail.

Bill walked with a great deal of spring to his step. He felt that he was getting somewhere now. He knew that Marcia was what he had thought her to be. She was a good kid, frightened to death by this deadly jungle and this wholesale slaughter, trying to make the world believe that she was not afraid.

What a hell of a shock, thought Bill, it must have been when they told her he had killed her Dad. No wonder she had given him the devil.

He took the smaller trails into the brush. Once or twice a lizard rattled the bushes ahead of him, and several times he had a bad scare when some night bird dived close to his head.

Somewhere along here he expected to meet up with the troopers. They would hardly fail to send out the word ahead of him. After all, hadn't he supposedly tried to ruin Big Business for Maracaibo?

Bill picked up el Opio *(and* el Opio *wasn't a very small man at all) and threw him across the saddle.*

He came out unexpectedly upon a main road. He hung back in the brush, looking up and down the dark length, fully expecting to receive a slug any moment. But the silence of the night reassured him.

"Hell," said Bill, "I'm tired of walking anyway."

Deliberately he sat down in the protection of a palm and waited. Very soon, he knew, the truck carrying his new rotary drill would come purring up this road. When that came, he would see just how much luck he had left.

He waited for an hour and a half without seeing any sign of life upon the highway. He wanted a cigarette but he didn't dare light one for fear the red glow would be spotted somewhere.

At last he heard a rumbling roar and saw the twin headlights roll around a curve. He walked out into the road and held up his hand.

The driver stamped on the brakes and leaned out of his cab, his eyes like marbles.

"Bill Murphy," gasped the driver. "I thought . . ."

"You thought a lot of things," said Bill. "Pull over to the side for a moment and I'll be right with you."

Bill undid *el Opio,* tied him up again, and loaded him into the back of the truck. He covered the man up with a mass of cables.

Sitting down on the tailgate, Bill said, "Okay, buddy, shove along. And if anybody should ask you, you don't know me, never seen me, and wouldn't like me if you did."

"But I thought the cavalry . . ."

"You thought nothing of the kind," said Bill, carefully building a cigarette. "And if you should happen to say anything if the cavalry stops you, maybe you might not get well very quick."

"But if they ask me where I'm taking this stuff and I tell them to Camp Chico, they'll make me go back."

Bill rubbed a match in his hair to dry it, put his sun hat on again and said, "Tell them you're taking it to Camp Jaguar."

"Okay," said the driver, doubtfully.

The man climbed into the cab again and started the engine. Bill's pony came up to the tailgate but Bill shoved him away. Plenty of time to pick up the horse later.

The truck rolled along for fifteen minutes without anything unusual occurring. And then the brakes squealed.

Bill stared ahead and saw five troopers standing their horses across the highway in a very determined fashion. Bill dived under a pile of cables.

Herrero was there, as this was the main traffic artery to the fields. Herrero looked very mad when he drew in alongside the cab and snarled at the driver.

"Have you seen anything of *señor* Murphy?"

"No," said the driver.

Herrero relaxed. "You are very fortunate, young man. *Señor* Murphy and I have an engagement here and he is late. By the way, young man, where are you going with this truck?"

"Camp Jaguar," said the driver.

"Camp Jaguar?" said Herrero. "Why, that might be very dangerous. Equipment for the wells, eh?"

"Yes. A rotary drill."

Lugarteniente Herrero was nothing if not polite. He beamed upon the driver and waved toward the brush. "You, Cueto, take four men and see that it gets to Camp Jaguar safely. We'll take care of your horses. You see," he added to the driver, "this *señor* Murphy may go there to make trouble. In fact, when I am relieved here, I am going there myself. The so beautiful *señorita* Stewart may be expecting me."

When he said that, Herrero wiped his hand across the welt over his eyes and grinned.

The five soldiers climbed aboard and the truck rolled off in the direction of Camp Jaguar—where some eighty drillers, Indians and killers in general, would like to see *señor* Bill Murphy without delay.

CHAPTER NINE

When the Cables Are Moved

L YING under the coils of heavy cable, jolted against unyielding machinery, Bill began to have doubts about the wisdom of his plan. He could hear the soldiers talking about him above the engine's roar, and the things they said were not exactly promising.

Cueto's heavy voice was heard to say, "This fellow, he has the greatest amount of brass. He comes down into town quite as if nothing in the world was there to stop him. He comes down and pretends to be the greatest man in town—excepting *lugarteniente* Herrero—and fools everybody."

The driver muttered something and Cueto expanded.

"But then we find this man Jorge Henderson lying along a path. We find somebody has stuck a knife into him—so! And right away, *lugarteniente* Herrero turns to me and he says, 'Cueto, you have a vast amount of training along this line, and I am asking for your opinion, Cueto, as you are the best sergeant I have ever had. What do you think about this, Cueto?'

"And so I said, '*Lugarteniente*, it appears that someone has made an attack on this man and I think that that man—the one who attacked him—was no other than that bloodthirsty renegade, Murphy.'

"And *lugarteniente* Herrero thinks and he says, 'Cueto, I

knew I could depend upon you as I always have.' And then he says, '*Por Dios,* did you not tell me that this Jorge Henderson was in the city?'

"Then I says, 'That is the point, *lugarteniente.* That is the point. He could not have been in the city and out here getting knifed at the same time.'

"And so the *lugarteniente* says, 'I think you are right. Perhaps we had better locate this impostor.' And so we did and what did we find? We found that I had been right in the first place. It *was* this Murphy.

"And so we tried to catch him, but he has the devil on his side and he got away from us, but we have the patrols out and the minute we lay eyes upon him, bango! He's a dead man!"

"You mean," said the driver, "that you'll shoot . . . shoot him in cold b-b-b-blood?"

"We are not afraid of him," said Cueto, proudly.

"No indeed," said another soldier. "I've got my sights all set for him. When the *lugarteniente* says shoot on sight, I shoot on sight, eh, Sergeant?"

"That's it," said the sergeant. "We aren't afraid of anybody, much less this murdering *jacaré,* Murphy."

The truck rolled on through the darkness and presently turned off into a mud-slimed, brush-lined trail which led up toward Camp Jaguar.

For expedience, a horse was best. Trucks had a nasty habit of getting bogged down and when they did that, you had to get out and remove all manner of heavy gear, unbog the truck and load the gear again.

Bill lay there sweating under the cables and hoped they wouldn't get into a mudhole this night.

They went slowly, evidently because the driver didn't want Bill Murphy to play this shooting-on-sight trick when they got into Jaguar. The driver probably hoped they would bog down, forgetting that the instant they did, Bill would be uncovered.

The truck rolled slower and slower. The sky began to glow up ahead. They were getting near Camp Jaguar.

Bill tensed himself for a dash the instant they stopped. Maybe the troopers' guns would stick in their holsters or something. Maybe there would be some excitement and he wouldn't be noticed.

Meantime they still had another kilometer to travel, the worst kilometer of all. The mud was so thick, it had a creamy quality when you beat it up. Pools of water lay in the jungle trail, ready and waiting for the unwary wheel. The driver slowed down again.

"Faster," said Bill, but he said it to himself. Trucks bogged faster when you slowed down. Was there no hope for it?

A rear wheel spun for a moment without picking up traction. The body lurched drunkenly and the truck slid back into the hole.

Bill gave a weary sigh and prepared to do battle.

Cueto climbed out with several grunts and looked the situation over with his flashlight.

"It's pretty deep," said Cueto.

"Too deep," agreed the driver.

"Do we have to unload?" said Cueto, warily. "We could get some of the Jaguar men. . . ."

The driver's words choked in his throat. "Ugh, blurg . . . ah . . . I don't think . . ."

The flashlight played over the load for the space of a minute. Bill could see the beams of it coming down through the cables. If the sergeant noticed a stray foot or hand, it would be just too bad.

Well, thought Bill, he wouldn't ever be able to explain to Marcia now. They'd unload this gear and that would be that. If shoot-on-sight orders had really been issued, it was all over. A Latin soldier likes nothing more.

Cueto gave orders for one of the men to go up to camp and Bill could hear the boots squishing away from there. Cueto sat down on the tailgate and smoked a cigarette. The driver walked up and down, up and down, and didn't even notice that he was wading through a deep pool.

"Keep a sharp lookout," said Cueto, to his three remaining men. "This fellow Murphy may try to come up this trail and you know your orders if he does."

Bill groaned silently. Poor Marcia. She was so sure she was right and that he had done these things attributed to him. It was tough, thought Bill. They'd had such a swell time when she'd been down here before. They'd gone riding and swimming and dancing and she'd told him . . .

The men were coming back from Jaguar.

Bill heard Romano's voice. "But I tell you, we didn't order a rotary drill! We didn't say anything. Where is the driver?

What do you mean by this? Are you crazy? What is the idea calling us off shift to unload a truck, eh? What is the matter with these pigs of soldiers, eh?"

"We must have made a mistake," said the driver, miserably.

"Hmmmm, a mistake," said Romano, scornfully. "That Stewart woman came back an hour ago and she didn't order this drill. She hasn't any brains as the good lord will testify, but she knows better than to order something we do not need."

Bill's hopes began to soar. Maybe they would refuse to unload the thing after all. Maybe they'd go back to camp and forget about it and maybe the soldiers would go with them.

They argued bitterly about it for some time and then Romano said, "Well, we cannot have you on this trail. We cannot do that. Turn around and go back to Maracaibo."

"I can't turn around here," said the driver.

"Then go up to camp. . . ."

"But we're bogged down, I tell you. You've got to unload the t-t . . . I mean . . . I'll see . . . see if I . . . if I can't b-b-b-b-back the thing out."

He tried but it was no use. The heavy load only made the wheel sink deeper.

"We'll unload it," snapped Romano peevishly, playing his flash over the load. "Here, you men, start on those cables."

The cables were jerked toward the tailgate. Bill hauled at them and tried to keep covered up. He couldn't fight off all these armed men. The instant they sighted him . . .

"¡Por Dios!" cried Cueto. "Look! Look! A hand! See!"

The men about the truck yelled and came closer, hauling at the cables.

"There's a foot!" cried Romano. "Pull him out of there. It's that Murphy! Pull him out of there and shoot him, quick!"

The cables jarred again and the soldiers gave a mighty heave.

Then there was a moment's silence.

Cueto roared, "What are you doing in there?"

Romano snapped, *"El Opio!"*

The soldiers grabbed the luckless gow-eater and hauled him down to the ground. But *el Opio* was bound and gagged, a fact which amazed them all.

"How did he get in here?" demanded Cueto of the driver.

"Somebody . . . somebody must have hid him," said the driver.

"Hid him," cried Romano. "Well, let him go. He's harmless."

"No," said Cueto, definitely. "I think I smell a mice."

"But what can you do with *him*?" protested Romano.

"I think we take him up to camp right away," said Cueto. "This man is undoubtedly in the pay of *señor* Murphy. This man is a hired assassin and I think the *lugarteniente* will thank me if I have him here for questioning."

"But my dear sergeant," said Romano, changing his tone completely, "I think you will be wasting your time by questioning . . ."

"I know what I am doing," roared Cueto. "You think you are smarter than the police, eh? You think you can outwit the cavalry. We take him to camp and question him."

They were so startled by their find that they completely forgot about the truck until somebody noticed that the driver was no longer present. This also mystified them greatly.

But with the driver gone, the truck meant nothing to them. They marched up the road bearing *el Opio* between them.

CHAPTER TEN

Fire Burns Them Down

BILL slid quietly out of the truck, threw off the safety catch of his rifle, inspected his revolver and walked off the road into the thick brush.

Bill had an idea, and, being Irish, when he got an idea nothing short of sudden death could shake it out of him. He had heard that conversation between Cueto and Romano and he had drawn himself a conclusion which, if Romano had suspected it, would have resulted in a wholesale search of Venezuela by every man Romano could beg, borrow or steal.

With that fixed idea in mind, Bill walked silently into Camp Jaguar.

Here the brush was no longer thick. The oil had attended to that, killing most of the growing things until the earth was as bare as Dad Lacey's bald head.

A plume of flame was shooting skyward, giving the night a macabre air by casting the derrick shadows ten times the lengths of the derricks themselves.

Several rigs were working, walking beams—great black arms saluting over and over. Men were moving through the maze of silhouettes, going about their jobs as though it had been bright day. The driller is a nocturnal beast in the tropics because it is cooler at night.

And besides, when two million cubic feet of natural gas comes out of the ground in a single day, and when you have to light it to keep on living and breathing, it is hard to tell the difference between high noon and midnight.

Steam, walking beams, drills, threshing cables, voices and roaring engines made a melody so commonplace that Bill felt he walked in the deepest of silence.

He made no try at slipping from door to door, from shack to shack. He was far too big for that. He walked in the shadow of a building as though he had urgent business there—as, indeed, he had.

Pressing his face against a dirty rectangle of glass, Bill saw that they had *el Opio* in a chair. *El Opio* was not so tall, sitting there. In fact he was very frightened. Cueto was roaring questions at him in rapid-fire order, volleys at a time. *El Opio* was too stunned to answer.

Or maybe *el Opio* saw the look Romano was giving him over Cueto's shoulder. *El Opio* grew shorter twenty-five feet at a time and Cueto grew taller in proportion. Nothing so invigorates the vocabulary of a trooper in Venezuela as an abject subject.

Finally, Cueto stomped out. "I am going to call Maracaibo with your office phone. There is something to this, *señor*." He slammed the door and Romano went into action.

Romano whipped *el Opio* out of the chair, snatched him up by his tattered shirt and spat deliberately into the craven face.

"You have killed on order before, you have your orders

now. I had thought to do something better with this Stewart woman. It is too late for that, you understand. You take this!"

He shoved a knife, hilt first, into *el Opio*'s hand. *El Opio* stared at it and then looked up at Romano. Romano pulled several black pills from his pocket and *el Opio* gobbled them.

Then a magical thing happened. *El Opio* grew first by inches, then by feet. Of course, this was occasioned by the fact that he was merely straightening his warped spine, but the effect was something to behold.

"I am one hundred feet tall," announced *el Opio*, a deadly glitter in his small black eyes. "I am a hundred feet tall and I will slide this knife into her back."

"Bueno," said Romano, and shoved *el Opio* out the door.

Bill ducked. He headed straight for Marcia's hut, heedless of the light. He couldn't avoid it and so he took it. There were many drillers there. Perhaps he could get by without . . .

Cueto was coming out of the office and he almost collided with Bill. Cueto tried to yell. Bill wrapped the muzzle of his gun around Cueto's ear and walked on toward the shack.

Another shadow was coming. A weird thing, with a shadow beside it on stilts. *El Opio,* knife in hand, was on his way.

Bill heard a car through the din of beams and drills. He heard it although the sound was almost lost. Someone was turning in from the main road. He heard a group of horses coming.

He threw open Marcia's door and slammed it behind him.

Marcia had been sitting at the table, head bent, eyes unseeing, over a stack of reports. She glanced up and stiffened.

"Bill! My God!"

Bill took hold of her wrist and walked across the room. There was another room beyond. He pulled her into it. He glanced about for the door and headed for it.

"We've got to get out of here," said Bill. "They're planning to murder you."

Marcia had offered no resistance. She was too stunned. She had believed that Bill was dead.

"Why . . ." said Marcia, "Why did you . . . ?"

"I had to get up here somehow, didn't I?" said Bill.

He opened the door and then slammed it quickly. He had caught a glimpse of Herrero in the midst of a cavalry troop. He heard the front door open.

"Listen," said Bill. "And don't interrupt. First thing, I love you. Second thing, we're both in the middle of a mess. This goes deeper than we think. I'm going to see it settled right now, if I can. Marcia, look up here at me. You never really believed that I did these things, did you?"

"No . . . But Romano and O'Brien saw you . . ."

"I thought that was it. Now, if I didn't, you still love me. Right? And nothing's changed?"

"Oh . . . Bill."

The shadow was standing in the doorway. The knife was balanced neatly between its thumb and index finger.

Bill fired from the hip.

El Opio went down in a cloud of swirling smoke, his arm shattered. He gripped it and stared blankly at Bill.

Fists were hammering on the door, boots were trying to kick it in.

El Opio *went down in a cloud of swirling smoke, his arm shattered. He gripped it and stared blankly at Bill.*

"Open this door!" bawled Herrero.

Bill picked up Marcia and ran to the front entrance. He slammed the door open and sprinted out.

Romano was standing, half of him glowing red in the light of the gas plume. Romano crouched forward and whipped up his revolver.

Bill dodged as Romano fired. The slug tore a long furrow in the clay.

In answer to the shots, the whole field was coming. Bill looked around at the rushing shadows, undecided.

He did not know whether or not they would shoot if he had Marcia with him. He could not risk it. He put Marcia down.

"Get away from me," snapped Bill. He had his gun in his hand and he was leaning a little forward like a duelist. Herrero and his men were coming up. Cueto was running toward them.

The whole panorama was moving except Bill. He stood there and tried to get Marcia to leave him.

"You'll get shot," he pleaded. "Step out."

Marcia's eyes were wide as she looked up at him. She was frowning a little, unable to realize just what he was doing, unable to believe, after these days of worry, of trying to convince herself that she hated him, that he would let himself be killed just on the chance that they would get excited and accidentally hit her.

Marcia swallowed hard. Her arms went up and about his neck.

"Bill," she said, softly.

Six regiments of infantry and one brigade of Marines could

not have whipped Bill at that moment. He put an arm around Marcia which almost crushed her.

Bill shot at Cueto and began to back up. He clipped one in the general direction of Herrero and Herrero stopped still.

Romano's finger was itching on the trigger but he did not dare shoot with Marcia there, too many were watching.

"Don't fire!" bawled Herrero. "You'll hit her!"

Bill was backing away, hoping they would not rush for another ten seconds. They were tightening the ring about him.

Above them a derrick loomed. Bill glanced up at it.

Marcia was still covering him but she had turned to face the soldiers. Her chin was held high and she almost smiled.

"Keep back," she ordered.

But the command acted in a different way. The men started their rush.

Bill picked up Marcia and grabbed the derrick ladder. He was fifteen feet off the ground before the men came close to him. One trooper started up but Bill tramped on his hands.

"Don't shoot," ordered Herrero above the din of shouts and steam and drills and roaring flame.

"I can climb it," protested Marcia.

"Shucks, I don't even know I've got you," said Bill with a grin.

As he went up he realized that this derrick had been recently used as a machine-gun tower. The platform on top could accommodate a crew of four and it was well sandbagged against a possible attack from the interior.

The crowd down below was yelling at each other, issuing and countermanding orders, railing because they could not shoot.

Bill lifted Marcia over the sandbags and then stepped up beside her. They crouched down on that dizzy perch and Bill leaned over the edge with a grin.

"Come on up," yelled Bill.

None of the troopers thought it a very good idea. Seventy-five feet was too far to fall when you were getting only a few *bolívars* a month for the job. Several of them, when ordered, resigned on the spot.

A car had somehow navigated the muddy roads and had somehow passed the stalled truck. It drove up to the crowd, and with some amazement, Bill found himself looking down upon the hat of George Henderson. True, the fellow's arm was swathed in splints, but he showed no signs of dying. Not right then, anyway.

The crowd began to talk in an ugly way. O'Brien was loudly declaiming any man who would hide behind a woman. It wasn't right and it wasn't the thing a gentleman like O'Brien would do. The man ought to step out and let himself get shot, that's what.

Herrero went into conference with George Henderson, listening with great respect, displaying the usual attitude shown Big Business by governmental powers in Latin America.

Then, somehow, a terrible thing happened. No one knew just how it came about, much less the sleek-haired Romano.

Tongues of flame leaped up the sides of the derrick, great, long licking things which devoured with a crackling, fiendish delight.

The derrick was burning under them.

The ladder was already eaten up to twenty feet from the ground.

Rolling smoke made Bill's voice husky. "I'm sorry, Marcia. I . . . I guess I'm pretty much a fool. Maybe if I'd stayed away and . . ."

"Hush," said Marcia, smoke getting into her eyes. "I understand now. It's too late, Bill, but maybe it's enough to know that . . ."

The geysering heat was intense. The tower began to tremble. In a moment it would go toppling down, sweeping through a sickening arc to the ground.

Bill stood up. "Okay, Romano. You've got me. But before . . ."

Something glinted in the light and Bill stared at it. Abruptly he whipped off his shirt, wrapped it around the stay and picked up Marcia.

"Hang on, kid," said Bill. "This is going to be a dizzy ride."

The guy-wire he had gripped with his shirt for hand protection led down from the top of the tower to the ground to steady the flimsy derrick against the high winds of the tropics.

Bill did not have time to test it. He hoped it would hold. With Marcia clinging to him, he swooped over to the edge of the platform.

The wire was straight and long. They went down it with the hot wind fanning them. The metal was burning through to Bill's palm, cutting through the flesh. Bill held on.

The ground came at them swiftly. Bill twisted himself so that he would hit first.

Behind them the tower swayed and began to lean. Suddenly it folded into itself in a shower of leaping sparks.

Bill hit with the speed of an express train. Somehow he kept Marcia from striking the ground too hard. The lights flashed in front of his face and went out.

He came to in a moment and tried to get up. Marcia had been thrust back away from him. Herrero was standing there now, gun in hand.

"Oh, so you're not dead," said Herrero. "A pity. But here is your *coup de grâce, señor* Murphy." He raised his revolver.

"Wait a minute," said Dad Lacey, shouldering through the crowd. He stopped in front of the startled Herrero and placed his palms on his twin gun butts. Dad spat carelessly on the toes of Herrero's shiny boots. "Don't be in a hurry, son," said Dad, wiping his mouth with his red flannel sleeve.

Herrero made a motion as if to fire, but Dad calmly held up his hand.

"Don't git careless, leftenant. Look over there."

The crowd parted with great swiftness. In the shadow of a shack they could see Edwards seated upon a machine-gun tripod. Edwards was very calm about it. He gave the air of not caring whether he shot or not. It all depended upon Dad's orders.

From the maze of derricks, men came walking. O'Malley and all the rest were there, even Ching, the cook, carrying an ancient fowling piece, followed faithfully by four cats.

The Camp Chico men sauntered up and began to relieve men of their guns and knives with a somewhat bored air.

Bill sat up and looked at Dad with great admiration.

90

"Nothin' to it," said Dad. "Your horse came home and you wasn't on it so we figured you might be here, and here you was. By the way," said Dad, offhand, "you see anything wrong with me?"

Bill stared at him and then saw that Dad was covered with thick black scum.

"My God!" screamed Bill. "Oil! You don't mean . . ."

"Look at the men," said Dad.

Bill and Herrero and Romano and Henderson all looked and saw that the men were smeared with oil too.

"Gusher," said Dad. "We didn't have time to cap the damned thing—beggin' your pardon, Miss."

But Marcia wasn't noticing such a minor affair as "damn." She was looking at Bill and laughing, and then looking at Dad and laughing at him and very soon a lot of the Camp Chico men were laughing with her.

Bill went over to Romano. Somebody had brought *el Opio* out of the hut and *el Opio* began to talk when he saw the look Bill gave him.

El Opio stood there in the glare of the burning plume and the derrick and talked louder and louder.

Romano tried to shut him up, but could not. George Henderson tried to shut him up, but George Henderson was not impressive at all there in the midst of brawny drillers. Somehow it takes a desk to make a Big Business man.

El Opio, well wound up by now, told them that Romano was the man that hired him to murder Miguel because Miguel knew too much to be bookkeeper at Jaguar. Romano had told him to murder old man Stewart and *el Opio* was a man who took orders to heart. Romano had told him to track Bill Murphy and *el Opio*, needing a pill, had made a mistake, but not a bad one because . . .

"So you're the ——— that knifed me!" yelled Henderson, shaking his fist under *el Opio*'s nose.

"Not so fast," said Bill, calmly. "Not so fast, Henderson. You know," he added in a whisper straight into Henderson's ear, "I wouldn't be a bit surprised but what you paid Romano in the first place."

Henderson turned very pale at that. He began to shake and his cheeks and eyes sank in.

"In fact," whispered Bill, "I *know* you did and I think we'd better give you your trial right here in front of Herrero and . . ."

Marcia was the only one close enough to hear. She looked at Bill and then at Henderson.

"Listen," said Henderson. "You've brought in a gusher. You've got a working well and your concession is safe. Listen here, Murphy . . ."

"Mr. Murphy to you."

"Listen, Mr. Murphy, I am prepared to pay you top prices for your land."

"Sure you will," said Bill. "But you wanted to save a million out of it for yourself and you set Romano and *el Opio* on Stewart to wipe him out because he wouldn't deal with you. Then, because I was over the main part of the oil lake, you wanted to get me in bad and get me jailed or killed so you could get my concession. You wanted the rest of the coin to yourself and you were going to gyp your company, the government and the rest of us for a few dirty dollars. Well, you can keep them."

"Listen, Mr. Murphy," pleaded Henderson, almost on his knees. "I'll do anything, anything . . . but . . . but please, please don't say anything. I . . . I'll buy your land for a million dollars cash."

"No," said Bill.

"I . . . I'll give you a million and a half."

"Okay," said Bill, "IF you'll buy the Stewart property for the same price."

"But I . . . I can't!"

"You can," said Bill, calmly building a cigarette.

Marcia intervened. "Bill! You've no right to sell. This is your life, Bill. Down here in the oil fields. You can't give it up. I know that. If you've got a gusher . . ."

"Marcia," said Bill, "you'd never be happy here. You hate this place. I'll find another field. I'll find something else back in your country. Shucks, with three million between us . . ."

Henderson was nervously fixing his fountain pen. It was significant of his wish to get these properties, that he had contracts with him. He had a checkbook and he had everything he needed. He wrote very steadily, using O'Malley's obliging back for a desk.

Bill took the check and dried it. "You've got a good buy, Henderson, and now, seeing that it's most dawn, let's all go down to Maracaibo and attend a party."

"A party?" said Marcia, blankly.

"Yeah," said Bill, "a wedding."

Dad Lacey whooped and the Camp Jaguar men cheered and even the troopers, now that they had things fairly straight, were quite willing to drink Bill's whisky.

They went in a mass down the trail toward the town.

Dad Lacey was telling Bill about it: how he'd fished up the wrench and how they'd drilled about two hundred feet more and how the oil had come up and smacked them in the face and how . . .

Dad stopped his monologue and dropped back. He spat reflectively into the brush, barely missing Herrero, but Herrero didn't seem to mind. He offered Dad a cigar. A nice, fresh cigar, straight out of Havana.

Dad looked at it reflectively and then bit it in two. "Uhuh," said Dad, philosophically, after studying Herrero a moment. "Uhuh, I guess I'm right after all." He chewed thoughtfully and said, "But three million makes you Big Business all right, and I guess me and Bill—and Marcia (I always said she was a good girl at heart)—just can't do no wrong, not ever, any more."

Dad grinned about that.

Story Preview

Story Preview

NOW that you've just ventured through one of the captivating tales in the Stories from the Golden Age collection by L. Ron Hubbard, turn the page and enjoy a preview of *The Bold Dare All.* Join Army Lieutenant Lee Briscoe as he locks horns with the sadistic master of a slave-labor island in the Celebes Sea of Southeast Asia. Complicating Lee's plans is a gorgeous young woman who's been bargained off to the same island lord.

The Bold Dare All

THE sinuous length of the blacksnake whip threshed like a snake in agony upon the blazing coral sand.

Back and forth, back and forth, it left a crazy pattern of arcs and wiped out the prints of naked feet.

Eyes followed the lash, back and forth, as though the whip really was a snake with the powers of hypnotism.

High above the tatterdemalion crowd the spinning sun whipped down its quivers of molten arrows.

Palm fronds drooped in the windless heat. Where the sea plumed up from the outer reef rose lazy, rainbowed steam. Beyond lay the Celebes Sea, a glazed, heat-polished metallic sheet of scorching blue.

Inland loomed the mountains. Festering green tangles spread over the rough and jagged slopes like scum left by a receding tide.

The miserable huts along the shore crouched among the crawling vines, trying to hide their scaly thatch and blistered boards. From the horizon to the peaks, everything was harsh, brutal and ugly.

The men who stood in awful fascination were clad in tatters or not clad at all. Upon their gaunt and wasted features were stamped the hard-living histories of their lives.

Like the bleached bones of the sailing ship which rotted upon the coral sand, these men had been cast up by the sea and the sea did not want them back.

No one wanted them but Schwenk, and Schwenk wanted nothing but their physical abilities. He wanted their hands and their backs and he took them and broke them as he pleased. Schwenk needed them because he needed copra.

The blacksnake whip was still lashing, making a hissing sound as it moved. A hand, copper-plated by the sun, horny with work, battered with fighting, gripped the leather-sewn butt. The nails were dirty; the back of the hand was hairy.

Above the thick forearm clung a sweat-grimed sleeve. The throat of the shirt was ripped back, exposing a long, livid scar which was the handiwork of a certain native who had gone mad.

A native would have to be mad to attack Schwenk. This one was long ago cured of his mental disease. Buried to the ears in sand, honey smeared over his features, he had been abandoned to a tribe of ants who had mandibles sharp enough to go through ironwood.

Everyone was watching that whip. Schwenk's gloating eyes caressed the writhing length, up and down, up and down, measuring it with a blood-freezing expertness born of long, long practice.

Schwenk thrust his black tongue between his broken black teeth and moistened his lipless mouth. The bloated circle of his face lighted up. His flawless blue, bitterly cold killer eyes shifted suddenly to the back of the man.

The native moaned helplessly. His brown eyes were still on that moving lash. His hands were suspended high over his head, wrists lashed together, making his back muscles bulge beneath the chocolate-colored satin of his skin. He shivered.

Schwenk dug his heels into the white sand. He bent his body forward, dragged the lash back to its full ten feet of length.

Sssst! Crack!

Blood burbled up through the torn flesh and glistened in the sunlight.

Sssst! Crack!

The man screamed.

Sssst! Crack!

The crisscross pattern grew more complex and then began to blur. In a matter of seconds chunks of flesh were squared out and turned around and left dangling by small bits of skin.

It was impossible to see any pattern now. Only a dripping, red mass. Flies were swarming in upon it, leaping up and out of the way each time the whip struck, settling back when the lash drew away.

The natives in the crowd were staring and shaking. The two dozen white derelicts looked on unaffected.

But on the edge of the throng stood a man apart. He was not watching the lash. He was watching Schwenk with disdainful eyes, studying the hot satisfaction which blazed upon Schwenk's face at each crack of the whip.

Lee Briscoe had only been on Timba for two months. He had not yet had time to become a ragged scarecrow. He still pipe-clayed his helmet, he still polished his well-cut boots, he was still particular about the way his khaki breeches and shirts were starched.

The crowd knew nothing about him but they whispered that he was wanted by the law. No man would work for Schwenk of his own free will. Others held that Lee Briscoe had been an Army lieutenant and had murdered a soldier. But not one held the real clue as to why the man had chosen hellhole Timba for a retreat.

Lee Briscoe's eyes were clear and gray. His face was darkly burned. His cheekbones were high and prominent and his jaw was lean and firm. He was built wide at the shoulders and tapered off from there like a boxer.

Schwenk was beginning to sweat at his work, but that did not curtail his enjoyment of it in the least. He was just getting into good form when Lee Briscoe stepped into the clear space behind him and snatched the lash as it swung back.

Lee Briscoe threw the blacksnake thirty feet down toward the water, but he did not watch it go as the others did. He was looking straight at Schwenk.

Schwenk turned slowly. He looked at the tips of Briscoe's boots and then at the crown of Briscoe's helmet. Casually, not in the least excited, Schwenk put his hand on the heavy butt of his belted revolver.

"You got anything to say about it?" said Schwenk, carelessly. "Maybe you just forgot yourself. Maybe somebody told you I liked to be interrupted. That it?"

Lee Briscoe's words came slowly, with a drawl. "There isn't any reason to kill him. Finky was a good man."

102

"He's a thief," said Schwenk. "I've got five hundred natives on Timba. If they start stealing . . ."

"Finky wouldn't have stolen anything if you'd feed good rations. He was hungry. All he took was a can of salmon and a half-dozen biscuits. If he'd killed his partner, you wouldn't have had a word to say. That isn't justice, Schwenk."

Schwenk sneered at Briscoe, turned and barked at the men: "He's taking over the island, boys. Tip your hats to him. I said, tip your hats!"

Uneasily, the two dozen derelicts touched their fingers to their battered helmets and straws.

Schwenk faced Briscoe again, lipless mouth curling into a ghastly grin. "Now is there anything else you want, Briscoe? Maybe a Scotch and soda? WONG! Bring Briscoe a Scotch and soda!"

There came a full minute's silence and then Wong, opium-drugged, slant-eyed servant to Schwenk, came forth with the order on a tray.

"Drink it up," said Schwenk, hand on the butt of his gun. "Drink it up, Mr. Briscoe, because that's the last time you're ever going to drink anything on this earth. I'm going to murder you, Briscoe. Right here. And murder isn't pleasant. Here, don't mind me, drink up!"

Briscoe looked levelly at Schwenk and knew that the man meant every word he said. No man but Schwenk could carry a gun on Timba—except when the natives staged one of their frequent revolts.

Briscoe looked at the lacerated back of the unconscious

Finky. He told himself that it was worth it. He reached for the bottle and poured out a big slug of Scotch. Behind him, the derelicts moved out of the line of fire.

"To your health, Schwenk," said Briscoe, carelessly, seeming to look only at his glass.

To find out more about *The Bold Dare All* and how you can obtain your copy, go to www.goldenagestories.com.

Glossary

Glossary

STORIES FROM THE GOLDEN AGE *reflect the words and expressions used in the 1930s and 1940s, adding unique flavor and authenticity to the tales. While a character's speech may often reflect regional origins, it also can convey attitudes common in the day. So that readers can better grasp such cultural and historical terms, uncommon words or expressions of the era, the following glossary has been provided.*

Anvil Chorus: in reference to a piece of music, "The Troubadour," by Italian composer Giuseppe Verdi (1813–1901), that depicts Spanish gypsies striking their anvils at dawn and singing the praises of hard work, good wine and their gypsy women.

aquí mismo: (Spanish) right here.

bolívars: (Spanish) coins and the monetary unit of Venezuela.

boot: saddle boot; a close-fitting covering or case for a gun or other weapon that straps to a saddle.

caballeros: (Spanish) gentlemen.

carbines: short light rifles, originally used by soldiers on horses.

cárcel: (Spanish) jail.

Celebes Sea: a section of the western Pacific Ocean between the Indonesian island of Sulawesi (formerly known as Celebes), Borneo and the southern Philippines.

chivvied: knifed; stabbed.

concession: a grant extended by a government to permit a company to explore for and produce oil, gas or mineral resources within a strictly defined geographic area, typically beneath government-owned lands. The grant is usually awarded to a company in consideration for some type of bonus or license fee and royalty or production sharing provided to the host government for a specified period of time.

copra: the dried kernel or meat of the coconut from which coconut oil is obtained.

coup de grâce: (French) "blow of mercy"; a death blow intended to end the suffering of a wounded creature. It is often used figuratively to describe the last of a series of events that brings about the end of some entity.

coyote: used for a man who has the sneaking and skulking characteristics of a coyote.

derrick: oil derrick; the towerlike framework over an oil well or the like.

dray: a low, strong cart without fixed sides for carrying heavy loads.

el Opio: (Spanish) the opium.

¿Es usted el señor Jorge Henderson, verdad?: (Spanish) Are you really Mister George Henderson?

forty-five or **.45:** a handgun chambered to fire a .45-caliber cartridge and that utilizes the recoil or part of the force of the explosive to eject the spent cartridge shell, introduce a new cartridge, cock the arm and fire it repeatedly.

fowling piece: shotgun or scatter-gun; useful primarily for hunting birds and other small game.

French Guiana: a French colony of northeast South America on the Atlantic Ocean, established in the nineteenth century and known for its penal colonies (now closed). Cayenne is the capital and the largest city.

G-men: government men; agents of the Federal Bureau of Investigation.

gow: opium.

grandee: a nobleman of the highest rank in Spain or Portugal.

gusher: an oil well from which oil spouts without being pumped.

guy-wire: a tensioned cable designed to add stability to tall, narrow structures. One end of the cable is attached to the structure and the other is anchored to the ground at a set distance from the structure's base.

Havana: a seaport in and the capital of Cuba, on the northwest coast.

hunkie: an unskilled or semi-skilled worker. The term originated from Central European immigrants; i.e., Hungarian, Lithuanian, Slav or Pole.

jacaré: (Spanish) alligator.

jipijapa: (Spanish) a stemless palmlike plant of Central and South America, having long-stalked, fanlike leaves that are used to make hats. They are named after Jipijapa, a city of western Ecuador. A hat made from this is also called a *Panama, Montecristi* or simply straw hat.

Lake Maracaibo: an inlet of the Caribbean Sea in northwestern Venezuela. The largest natural lake in South America, it occupies an area of 5,130 square miles.

limonada: (Spanish) lemonade.

llaneros: (Spanish) literally *plainsmen*; Venezuelan and Columbian cowboys who were originally part Spanish and Indian.

lugarteniente: (Spanish) deputy lieutenant.

Maracaibo: the second largest city in Venezuela after the national capital. It is nicknamed "the land loved by the sun."

Navy Colt: the name of a line of revolvers originally produced by Samuel Colt (1814–1862). In order to attract Navy contracts, Colt used the expression *Navy* to indicate .36 caliber rather than the .44 caliber required by the Army.

octubre: (Spanish) October.

pipe-clayed: made clean and smart; pipe clay is a fine white clay used in whitening leather. It was at one time largely used by soldiers for making their gloves, accouterments and clothes look clean and smart.

pizen: poison.

Planter's Punch: a punch made with dark rum, light rum, lime juice, orange juice, pineapple juice and topped with soda.

por Dios: (Spanish) for God's sake.

prove: to establish, by drilling, trenching or other means, that a given deposit of a valuable substance exists and that its grade and dimensions equal or exceed some specified amounts.

Scheherazade: the female narrator of *The Arabian Nights,* who during one thousand and one adventurous nights saved her life by entertaining her husband, the king, with stories.

seep: a spot where water or petroleum trickles out of the ground to form a pool.

¿Señor, donde esta el chico?: (Spanish) Mister, where is the boy?

señorita: (Spanish) young lady.

Siberia: an extensive region in what is now the Russian Federation in northern Asia, extending from the Ural Mountains to the Pacific.

Sonora: a state in northwestern Mexico.

soup wagon: a wagon or truck used to haul liquid nitroglycerin.

Spanish Inquisition: the Inquisition in Spain, under state control from 1480 to 1834, marked by the extreme severity and cruelty of its proceedings in the sixteenth century.

spirit gum: a theatrical adhesive to apply wigs, beards and things of that nature.

Springfield: any of several types of rifle, named after Springfield, Massachusetts, the site of a federal armory that made the rifles.

sulfur candle: a candle used for fumigating and killing pests and fungal organisms.

tatterdemalion: raggedly dressed and unkempt.

Tengo una carta, señor: (Spanish) I have a letter, mister.

thirty-thirty or **.30-30:** Winchester model 1894 rifle that is chambered to fire a .30-30 cartridge, the first North American sporting cartridge designed for use with smokeless powder. The .30-30 is a .30-caliber cartridge that was originally loaded with 30 grains of the new smokeless powder, which is the source of its name.

tonto: (Spanish) fool; blockhead.

took to his heels: ran away.

Union Square: (also known as Union Square Park) an important and historic intersection in New York City. It was the site of a very large Communist demonstration in 1930 and has been home to the Communist Party's national headquarters. It was sometimes known as "Red Square" because Communist activists addressed crowds there.

ya lo creo: (Spanish) of course, naturally.

¿Y el señor **Murphy***?:* (Spanish) And Mister Murphy?

L. Ron Hubbard
in the Golden Age
of Pulp Fiction

*In writing an adventure story
a writer has to know that he is adventuring
for a lot of people who cannot.
The writer has to take them here and there
about the globe and show them
excitement and love and realism.
As long as that writer is living the part of an
adventurer when he is hammering
the keys, he is succeeding with his story.*

*Adventuring is a state of mind.
If you adventure through life, you have a
good chance to be a success on paper.*

*Adventure doesn't mean globe-trotting,
exactly, and it doesn't mean great deeds.
Adventuring is like art.
You have to live it to make it real.*

—*L. RON HUBBARD*

L. Ron Hubbard
and American
Pulp Fiction

B ORN March 13, 1911, L. Ron Hubbard lived a life at least as expansive as the stories with which he enthralled a hundred million readers through a fifty-year career.

Originally hailing from Tilden, Nebraska, he spent his formative years in a classically rugged Montana, replete with the cowpunchers, lawmen and desperadoes who would later people his Wild West adventures. And lest anyone imagine those adventures were drawn from vicarious experience, he was not only breaking broncs at a tender age, he was also among the few whites ever admitted into Blackfoot society as a bona fide blood brother. While if only to round out an otherwise rough and tumble youth, his mother was that rarity of her time—a thoroughly educated woman—who introduced her son to the classics of Occidental literature even before his seventh birthday.

But as any dedicated L. Ron Hubbard reader will attest, his world extended far beyond Montana. In point of fact, and as the son of a United States naval officer, by the age of eighteen he had traveled over a quarter of a million miles. Included therein were three Pacific crossings to a then still mysterious Asia, where he ran with the likes of Her British Majesty's agent-in-place

L. Ron Hubbard, left, at Congressional Airport, Washington, DC, 1931, with members of George Washington University flying club.

for North China, and the last in the line of Royal Magicians from the court of Kublai Khan. For the record, L. Ron Hubbard was also among the first Westerners to gain admittance to forbidden Tibetan monasteries below Manchuria, and his photographs of China's Great Wall long graced American geography texts.

Upon his return to the United States and a hasty completion of his interrupted high school education, the young Ron Hubbard entered George Washington University. There, as fans of his aerial adventures may have heard, he earned his wings as a pioneering barnstormer at the dawn of American aviation. He also earned a place in free-flight record books for the longest sustained flight above Chicago. Moreover, as a roving reporter for *Sportsman Pilot* (featuring his first professionally penned articles), he further helped inspire a generation of pilots who would take America to world airpower.

Immediately beyond his sophomore year, Ron embarked on the first of his famed ethnological expeditions, initially to then untrammeled Caribbean shores (descriptions of which would later fill a whole series of West Indies mystery-thrillers). That the Puerto Rican interior would also figure into the future of Ron Hubbard stories was likewise no accident. For in addition to cultural studies of the island, a 1932–33

LRH expedition is rightly remembered as conducting the first complete mineralogical survey of a Puerto Rico under United States jurisdiction.

There was many another adventure along this vein: As a lifetime member of the famed Explorers Club, L. Ron Hubbard charted North Pacific waters with the first shipboard radio direction finder, and so pioneered a long-range navigation system universally employed until the late twentieth century. While not to put too fine an edge on it, he also held a rare Master Mariner's license to pilot any vessel, of any tonnage in any ocean.

Yet lest we stray too far afield, there is an LRH note at this juncture in his saga, and it reads in part:

"I started out writing for the pulps, writing the best I knew, writing for every mag on the stands, slanting as well as I could."

To which one might add: His earliest submissions date from the summer of 1934, and included tales drawn from true-to-life Asian adventures, with characters roughly modeled on British/American intelligence operatives he had known in Shanghai. His early Westerns were similarly peppered with details drawn from personal

Capt. L. Ron Hubbard in Ketchikan, Alaska, 1940, on his Alaskan Radio Experimental Expedition, the first of three voyages conducted under the Explorers Club flag.

experience. Although therein lay a first hard lesson from the often cruel world of the pulps. His first Westerns were soundly rejected as lacking the authenticity of a Max Brand yarn (a particularly frustrating comment given L. Ron Hubbard's Westerns came straight from his Montana homeland, while Max Brand was a mediocre New York poet named Frederick Schiller Faust, who turned out implausible six-shooter tales from the terrace of an Italian villa).

Nevertheless, and needless to say, L. Ron Hubbard persevered and soon earned a reputation as among the most publishable names in pulp fiction, with a ninety percent placement rate of first-draft manuscripts. He was also among the most prolific, averaging between seventy and a hundred thousand words a month. Hence the rumors that L. Ron Hubbard had redesigned a typewriter for faster keyboard action and pounded out manuscripts on a continuous roll of butcher paper to save the precious seconds it took to insert a single sheet of paper into manual typewriters of the day.

That all L. Ron Hubbard stories did not run beneath said byline is yet another aspect of pulp fiction lore. That is, as publishers periodically rejected manuscripts from top-drawer authors if only to avoid paying top dollar, L. Ron Hubbard and company just as frequently replied with submissions under various pseudonyms. In Ron's case, the list

---

A MAN OF MANY NAMES

Between 1934 and 1950, L. Ron Hubbard authored more than fifteen million words of fiction in more than two hundred classic publications. To supply his fans and editors with stories across an array of genres and pulp titles, he adopted fifteen pseudonyms in addition to his already renowned L. Ron Hubbard byline.

Winchester Remington Colt
Lt. Jonathan Daly
Capt. Charles Gordon
Capt. L. Ron Hubbard
Bernard Hubbel
Michael Keith
Rene Lafayette
Legionnaire 148
Legionnaire 14830
Ken Martin
Scott Morgan
Lt. Scott Morgan
Kurt von Rachen
Barry Randolph
Capt. Humbert Reynolds

---

included: Rene Lafayette, Captain Charles Gordon, Lt. Scott Morgan and the notorious Kurt von Rachen—supposedly on the lam for a murder rap, while hammering out two-fisted prose in Argentina. The point: While L. Ron Hubbard as Ken Martin spun stories of Southeast Asian intrigue, LRH as Barry Randolph authored tales of romance on the Western range—which, stretching between a dozen genres is how he came to stand among the two hundred elite authors providing close to a million tales through the glory days of American Pulp Fiction.

L. Ron Hubbard, circa 1930, at the outset of a literary career that would finally span half a century.

In evidence of exactly that, by 1936 L. Ron Hubbard was literally leading pulp fiction's elite as president of New York's American Fiction Guild. Members included a veritable pulp hall of fame: Lester "Doc Savage" Dent, Walter "The Shadow" Gibson, and the legendary Dashiell Hammett—to cite but a few.

Also in evidence of just where L. Ron Hubbard stood within his first two years on the American pulp circuit: By the spring of 1937, he was ensconced in Hollywood, adopting a Caribbean thriller for Columbia Pictures, remembered today as *The Secret of Treasure Island*. Comprising fifteen thirty-minute episodes, the L. Ron Hubbard screenplay led to the most profitable matinée serial in Hollywood history. In accord with Hollywood culture, he was thereafter continually called

The 1937 Secret of Treasure Island, *a fifteen-episode serial adapted for the screen by L. Ron Hubbard from his novel,* Murder at Pirate Castle.

upon to rewrite/doctor scripts—most famously for long-time friend and fellow adventurer Clark Gable.

In the interim—and herein lies another distinctive chapter of the L. Ron Hubbard story—he continually worked to open Pulp Kingdom gates to up-and-coming authors. Or, for that matter, anyone who wished to write. It was a fairly unconventional stance, as markets were already thin and competition razor sharp. But the fact remains, it was an L. Ron Hubbard hallmark that he vehemently lobbied on behalf of young authors—regularly supplying instructional articles to trade journals, guest-lecturing to short story classes at George Washington University and Harvard, and even founding his own creative writing competition. It was established in 1940, dubbed the Golden Pen, and guaranteed winners both New York representation and publication in *Argosy.*

But it was John W. Campbell Jr.'s *Astounding Science Fiction* that finally proved the most memorable LRH vehicle. While every fan of L. Ron Hubbard's galactic epics undoubtedly knows the story, it nonetheless bears repeating: By late 1938, the pulp publishing magnate of Street & Smith was determined to revamp *Astounding Science Fiction* for broader readership. In particular, senior editorial director F. Orlin Tremaine called for stories with a stronger *human element.* When acting editor John W. Campbell balked, preferring his spaceship-driven tales,

Tremaine enlisted Hubbard. Hubbard, in turn, replied with the genre's first truly *character-driven* works, wherein heroes are pitted not against bug-eyed monsters but the mystery and majesty of deep space itself—and thus was launched the Golden Age of Science Fiction.

The names alone are enough to quicken the pulse of any science fiction aficionado, including LRH friend and protégé, Robert Heinlein, Isaac Asimov, A. E. van Vogt and Ray Bradbury. Moreover, when coupled with LRH stories of fantasy, we further come to what's rightly been described as the foundation of every modern tale of horror: L. Ron Hubbard's immortal *Fear*. It was rightly proclaimed by Stephen King as one of the very few works to genuinely warrant that overworked term "classic"—as in: *"This is a classic tale of creeping, surreal menace and horror. . . . This is one of the really, really good ones."*

L. Ron Hubbard, 1948, among fellow science fiction luminaries at the World Science Fiction Convention in Toronto.

To accommodate the greater body of L. Ron Hubbard fantasies, Street & Smith inaugurated *Unknown*—a classic pulp if there ever was one, and wherein readers were soon thrilling to the likes of *Typewriter in the Sky* and *Slaves of Sleep* of which Frederik Pohl would declare: *"There are bits and pieces from Ron's work that became part of the language in ways that very few other writers managed."*

And, indeed, at J. W. Campbell Jr.'s insistence, Ron was regularly drawing on themes from the Arabian Nights and so introducing readers to a world of genies, jinn, Aladdin and Sinbad—all of which, of course, continue to float through cultural mythology to this day.

At least as influential in terms of post-apocalypse stories was L. Ron Hubbard's 1940 *Final Blackout*. Generally acclaimed as the finest anti-war novel of the decade and among the ten best works of the genre ever authored—here, too, was a tale that would live on in ways few other writers

imagined. Hence, the later Robert Heinlein verdict: "Final Blackout *is as perfect a piece of science fiction as has ever been written.*"

Like many another who both lived and wrote American pulp adventure, the war proved a tragic end to Ron's sojourn in the pulps. He served with distinction in four theaters and was highly decorated for commanding corvettes in the North Pacific. He was also grievously wounded in combat, lost many a close friend and colleague and thus resolved to say farewell to pulp fiction and devote himself to what it had supported these many years—namely, his serious research.

Portland, Oregon, 1943; L. Ron Hubbard captain of the US Navy subchaser PC 815.

But in no way was the LRH literary saga at an end, for as he wrote some thirty years later, in 1980:

"Recently there came a period when I had little to do. This was novel in a life so crammed with busy years, and I decided to amuse myself by writing a novel that was pure science fiction."

That work was *Battlefield Earth: A Saga of the Year 3000*. It was an immediate *New York Times* bestseller and, in fact, the first international science fiction blockbuster in decades. It was not, however, L. Ron Hubbard's magnum opus, as that distinction is generally reserved for his next and final work: The 1.2 million word *Mission Earth*.

> **Final Blackout**
> *is as perfect*
> *a piece of*
> *science fiction as*
> *has ever*
> *been written.*
>
> —Robert Heinlein

How he managed those 1.2 million words in just over twelve months is yet another piece of the L. Ron Hubbard legend. But the fact remains, he did indeed author a ten-volume *dekalogy* that lives in publishing history for the fact that each and every volume of the series was also a *New York Times* bestseller.

Moreover, as subsequent generations discovered L. Ron Hubbard through republished works and novelizations of his screenplays, the mere fact of his name on a cover signaled an international bestseller. . . . Until, to date, sales of his works exceed hundreds of millions, and he otherwise remains among the most enduring and widely read authors in literary history. Although as a final word on the tales of L. Ron Hubbard, perhaps it's enough to simply reiterate what editors told readers in the glory days of American Pulp Fiction:

He writes the way he does, brothers, because he's been there, seen it and done it!

THE STORIES FROM THE GOLDEN AGE

Your ticket to adventure starts here with the Stories from
the Golden Age collection by master storyteller L. Ron Hubbard.
These gripping tales are set in a kaleidoscope of exotic locales and brim
with fascinating characters, including some of the
most vile villains, dangerous dames and brazen heroes
you'll ever get to meet.

The entire collection of over one hundred and fifty stories is being
released in a series of eighty books and audiobooks.
For an up-to-date listing of available titles,
go to www.goldenagestories.com.

AIR ADVENTURE

Arctic Wings	*Man-Killers of the Air*
The Battling Pilot	*On Blazing Wings*
Boomerang Bomber	*Red Death Over China*
The Crate Killer	*Sabotage in the Sky*
The Dive Bomber	*Sky Birds Dare!*
Forbidden Gold	*The Sky-Crasher*
Hurtling Wings	*Trouble on His Wings*
The Lieutenant Takes the Sky	*Wings Over Ethiopia*

FAR-FLUNG ADVENTURE

SEA ADVENTURE

TALES FROM THE ORIENT

MYSTERY

FANTASY

Borrowed Glory   If I Were You
The Crossroads   The Last Drop
Danger in the Dark   The Room
The Devil's Rescue   The Tramp
He Didn't Like Cats

SCIENCE FICTION

The Automagic Horse   A Matter of Matter
Battle of Wizards   The Obsolete Weapon
Battling Bolto   One Was Stubborn
The Beast   The Planet Makers
Beyond All Weapons   The Professor Was a Thief
A Can of Vacuum   The Slaver
The Conroy Diary   Space Can
The Dangerous Dimension   Strain
Final Enemy   Tough Old Man
The Great Secret   240,000 Miles Straight Up
Greed   When Shadows Fall
The Invaders

WESTERN

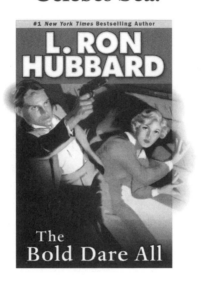

JOIN THE PULP REVIVAL
America in the 1930s and 40s

Pulp fiction was in its heyday and 30 million readers were regularly riveted by the larger-than-life tales of master storyteller L. Ron Hubbard. For this was pulp fiction's golden age, when the writing was raw and every page packed a walloping punch.

That magic can now be yours. An evocative world of nefarious villains, exotic intrigues, courageous heroes and heroines—a world that today's cinema has barely tapped for tales of adventure and swashbucklers.

Enroll today in the Stories from the Golden Age Club and begin receiving your monthly feature edition selected from more than 150 stories in the collection.

You may choose to enjoy them as either a paperback or audiobook for the special membership price of $9.95 each month along with FREE shipping and handling.

CALL TOLL-FREE: **1-877-8GALAXY**
(1-877-842-5299) OR GO ONLINE TO
www.goldenagestories.com
AND BECOME PART OF THE PULP REVIVAL!

Prices are set in US dollars only. For non-US residents, please call
1-323-466-7815 for pricing information. Free shipping available for US residents only.

Galaxy Press, 7051 Hollywood Blvd., Suite 200, Hollywood, CA 90028